A PROMISE
OF DIAMONDS

A Promise of Diamonds

A Patrick Dawlish Mystery

John Creasey *writing as*
Gordon Ashe

OPEN ROAD

INTEGRATED MEDIA
NEW YORK

ISBN: 978-1-5040-9812-0

This edition published in 2024 by Open Road Integrated Media, Inc.
180 Maiden Lane
New York, NY 10038
www.openroadmedia.com

A PROMISE
OF DIAMONDS

CHAPTER I

THE VIGIL

It was hot, so hot that the sun burned and dried everything out of the pale earth.

It was hot, so hot that the sun made a shimmering haze of silvery light which blinded man and beast, deluding them with promises of coolness and of water which were not there. In the town there were eleven houses, not really enough to be a town, but what else would one call it? Not a village, because there was no central place, no cluster of houses about a church; not even a road, only a track made by a few wheeled vehicles and fewer caterpillar tractors which had long since been driven off or had rotted away. The eleven houses were all within sight of one another; perhaps that created a unit large and cohesive enough to be called a town.

The place had a name: Kangarmie.

No one knew where the name had come from, and no one here now cared. The fact that no one cared revealed itself in the signpost on the 'road' near the first house. It said: 'K . . . rmie'; the rest of the letters had faded, sun-rotted, but for some odd reason the five remained, faint grey on a background that had once been white but was now parched-looking board like the dried skin of a mamba. Near it was a metal one which had withstood the heat better. It said: 'HELL', in big black letters on a faded yellow background. That was a great joke among the inhabitants of Kangarmie. A drunken truck driver had hit the metal, bending it and denting his cabin. He had so damaged the paint that the 'S' which should have been at the front of 'hell' was missing.

'Hell,' the inhabitants would say when in the right mood. 'Short for Kangarmie.'

It was difficult for outsiders to understand why the town still existed. True, it still sold petrol and provided a bath and food for travellers, but few passed through since the mine had closed down. Over in the derelict compound, where the mud huts stood the test of time as well if not better than the wood of the white houses, there were indications that over a hundred years ago Bantu mineworkers had once lived, laughing, eating, fighting, dancing, saving money to take home to the kraal. Beyond the compound, on the side of the hill, was a skeleton of what had once been the mine's superstructure, stark lengths of rusty iron which had taken on a kind of pattern, as if a drunken artist had tried to paint what wasn't there. The shaft of the mine was hidden, of course; in fact, the opening was boarded up to make sure that no one tried to go down into the bowels of the earth to find an illusory fortune. There had been gold, but the vein had been worked out in eleven short years and forgotten by most for twenty.

Yet Kangarmie still existed, its inhabitants showing a stubborn loyalty.

The few who did drive across this southern tip of the Kalahari Desert were grateful, for one could sleep as well as eat and drink and bath; but there were better routes across the desert, roads which led from somewhere to somewhere, not nowhere to nowhere. Occasionally an adventurous youngster came, following a road which should no longer have appeared on the map but which had never been taken off. Occasionally a safari passed this way, heading for Bushman country further north. Sometimes an expedition seeking the flora or the fauna, the flowers or the beasts, came and pitched camp and descended upon the café-cum-bottle-store-cum-garage. This, the biggest building in Kangarmie, was owned by Jacob Parkin and run by his wife, two sons, and one daughter-in-law. Parkin himself was always out in the desert or in the far-off hills, prospecting; sometimes he was away six months at a time.

Everyone in the other houses had some kind of reason for staying even though the reason made little sense to people who did not know the strange fascination that the desert could exert. There were the Ellises, the Longfellows, the du Toits, the Browns, the Forrests. . . .

Della Forrest had the best reason of any. She was waiting for her husband to come back. She had waited for a long time, for over two years.

The house she lived in was no more worthy of the name 'house' than Kangarmie was worthy of the name 'town'. It had two rooms, bedroom and living room, and a built-on kitchen. There was no piped water in Kangarmie; there never had been. There was practically no rain, either, so it was no hardship to go outside.

The unusual thing about Della Forrest's house was its spick-and-span appearance inside. Nothing could exist in that burning sun and look newly painted outside, and 'Promise' was no exception, but inside it put everyone else in the town to shame—or it would have, had there been any sense of pride in any other housewife there.

'She must be mad,' the neighbours would say, 'Keeping it ready for him to come home. He'll never come back.'

There were times when Della herself wondered if she was a little mad. This afternoon was one of the occasions.

She stood by the window, where the Venetian blinds were down and the slats made bars of fierce light and bars of dark shadow across her pale face. It was a nice face, not beautiful, but certainly not plain. She had fine hazel-coloured eyes and long lashes, a short nose, and rather full lips.

When she laughed, which wasn't often these days, her whole face lit up.

She was half frowning as she looked towards the hill, the skeleton of rusted steel, and the distance beyond. Even after all these months it was impossible for her to stand here without recalling the day when Nigel had left. She had stood at this very spot, watching the Land-Rover as it careered along the sandy track towards the hill. Her last glimpse had been of its silhouette, black against the sky, black as the steelwork was now. Suddenly it had appeared to topple over the edge and vanish. At the time and to this day she believed Nigel had waved, had imagined his right hand and arm outside of the truck, but she wasn't actually sure. Even now she reminded herself that she knew Nigel very well. The moment after he had kissed her and turned away his thoughts had been on where he was going, not on her. Oh, he loved her, but not with the kind of love she had for him; she was not everything that mattered in his life. There was always the thing he wanted on the other side of the hill, tomorrow's promise. When they had first met he had been an apprentice diamond-cutter at one of the mines, but the indoor life had palled on him, and the lure of prospecting had been too strong. He had been so sure he was right to leave his job. Day after day these memories passed through Della's mind, but they were seldom so oppressive as they were today. There was no special reason; it wasn't an anniversary, not even the same day of the week as he had left; it was Thursday, and he had left on a Monday.

'Give me two months, sweet, and I'll be back with a fortune in diamonds. That's a promise!'

Promise, promise, promise! At times she felt that she hated the word.

Della half turned—and then thought she saw a movement, a black speck, on the brow of the hill. Her heart leaped and began to beat sickeningly, but it was only a bird—a vulture, probably after some dead creature of the desert. She turned away from the window and stepped towards the door which led to the kitchen.

It opened.

'Oh!' she exclaimed, taken in fright. Then she saw the man beyond. 'Jeff, you scared me.'

'I was hoping I would,' the man said. 'Someone has to scare away the ghosts.'

'Jeff, please.'

He was a short, stocky man in the middle forties, twice her age. He had clear, rather deep-set blue eyes, a short nose, thin, fine fair hair. He wore a well-used bush jacket and shorts which were too long for him and made him look a little broad.

'Della,' he said, 'you've got to make yourself realise that he's never coming back.'

She did not answer.

'If you go on like this, you'll drive yourself crazy.' Jeff Mason went on. He had a hard, rather metallic voice. 'You'll do what everyone says you'll do.'

'Oh,' Della said quietly. 'And what does everyone say I'll do?'

'Della—'

'Tell me what they say.'

'Della, you know—'

'I'll know when you tell me,' Della said.

'You know as well as I do that everyone says you'll waste the whole of your life if you go on brooding like this.' Jeff took a step towards her, one arm outstretched. 'Give it up, Della. You've waited much longer than most women would. You're too young and to lovely to waste yourself on a memory.'

'I'm too young and too lovely to waste myself on a middle-aged widower who can't think beyond me wanting to go to bed with him.'

She meant it to hurt; she meant it to stop Jeff Mason from his ceaseless attempts to break down her resistance. She saw the colour ebb from his cheeks and the way the glow faded out of his eyes. She had hurt him all right. But he did not turn away, although his arm dropped to his side.

'One day you may need me,' he said. 'Then you may believe the truth—that I love you.'

She didn't speak. It was no use relenting, for that would encourage him more cruelly than she had wounded him.

'All I want is you to start living again,' Jeff went on. 'Whether you choose me or another man isn't important. The essential thing is for you to stop living for a ghost.'

He stood there long enough for the words to sink in, then swung around on his heel. The door between the two rooms swung to behind him, swayed, creaked, and fell silent. His footsteps sounded on the wooden floor of the stoep, then on the sandy gravel outside. She could hear the *crunch, crunch, crunch.* Suddenly she thought, 'I didn't hear him come in.'

She was puzzled, wondering how long he had been in the house. He knew it well. He had been a good friend of Nigel's. And no one in Kangarmie locked their doors by day, although a few did by night.

She recalled the hurt which had shown so starkly in his eyes but did not dwell on it. She had tried for so long to be gentle with him; hardness might make him realise that he had no hope. She turned to look out of the window again.

Her heart seemed to turn over, for someone *was* there, on the hill—near the very spot where Nigel had vanished. She began to breathe very heavily and felt as if she were unable to move.

A man was coming down the hill.

She saw him sway and stagger as if he could not keep his balance. He was tall and his figure was dark against the sandy grey of the hillside. She turned quickly, snatching a pair of binoculars from a table nearby. When she put them to her eyes her vision was blurred. She twisted the wheel for focus. Tiny shrubs showed up. Rocks showed vividly. A little outcrop appeared very dark.

The man came into her line of vision.

He *was* staggering. She could not see his face because he wore a big wide-brimmed hat, and the brim was low over his eyes, but she saw the old bush jacket he was wearing, the torn and tattered shorts.

Nigel?

It couldn't be, but it must be!

She thought desperately. 'Oh God, make it Nigel!'

She rushed towards the door and for the first time for months wished Jeff Mason were at hand. He could take her up the hill. She hadn't a car and couldn't walk fast enough.

What was the matter with her? Of course she could walk!

She snatched a broad-brimmed linen hat from a peg in the living room and hurried out. The binoculars were heavy in her right hand, knocking against her leg. Dust spurted from her footsteps. She was in the grip of a kind of panic, realised it, but could do nothing about it. It was like a nightmare. She was conscious of fear of waking to something more hideous, to the fear that she was wrong again.

She had run like this four times before. Each time she had been wrong. Three times there had been no one up there, only desert driftwood stirred by the wind. Once it had been an old man who lived like a ghoul in the ruins of the compound. Each time when she had run she had prayed that it was Nigel, although prayer had not come easily to her since she had been a child.

This time, oh God, it must be Nigel.

She saw old Mrs. Cratton on her stoep, swinging a ceaseless to and fro in her big rocking chair. Mrs. Cratton was only twenty yards away. She was knitting some interminable garment.

'Come here, gel!' she called.

Della ran on.

Cranky, querulous, half-dead Granny Cratton, who lived here because she had no other place to go, thought Della crazily.

She felt mad. For a few minutes a nearer rise in the land hid the hill from her, and she could not see whether there remained any hope that she was right. She was gasping for breath and for the first time became fully aware of the deadly heat. It burned from the sky and it burned from the sand of the earth. It dried her body and it dried her mouth and lips. The sand was thicker here, and running was more difficult; her feet kept on slipping, slithering. As she neared the top of the rising land, she fell and hurt her knee. She cried out involuntarily but staggered back to her feet, the binoculars banging her bruised knee, and ran on. The moment she could see the hill again she stopped to stare, straining her eyes desperately. She *thought* the man was still there. She thought—why couldn't she see more clearly?

The binoculars were a dead weight on the end of the strap;

she had forgotten that she had them with her and could not understand why the moving figure on the hill seemed so small.

Then she remembered and raised the glasses too quickly, catching her eyes. One eye watered. It was as if she were fated not to see. She dashed the tears of pain away and forced herself to be steady. At last the binoculars were properly focused on the man.

She could not see the face, could not be positive that it was Nigel; but it was a tall, very thin man, staggering down the slope, making little spurts of dust with every step. He looked as if he had no control of his legs and would soon fall.

The ground was rising now; it was uphill all the way and even more difficult for her to run. The backs of her legs ached badly.

Suddenly she was aware of the engine of a car not far behind. She did not turn to look but thought, Jeff, thank God. The engine drew nearer and much louder, knocking badly. The stink of oil and petrol wafted towards her in the wind. Then the nose of Jeff's old black Studebaker drew level with her. She stopped, Jeff was leaning forward and opening the door. He did not speak. She clambered in and dropped down beside him, gasping. He leaned across and pulled the door. It slammed. His arm touched her breasts and seemed to linger, then he put both hands on the wheel. The doors rattled and the engine seemed to shake the whole car, it clattered so.

Jeff still didn't speak. When she looked at him he was staring straight ahead, lips set tightly, big square jaw thrust forward. Della knew what he was thinking, that this wasn't Nigel, that she was wrong again.

Fear that he was right gripped her like icy fingers in the burning desert.

CHAPTER II

THE REWARD

Soon they were only a few hundred yards from the staggering man. The engine was snarling and missing on at least two cylinders. Dust smeared the windscreen so that it was not easy to see out. There was little need for the glasses now, for the big brimmed hat was still over the man's face.

Jeff said gruffly, 'If you hadn't seen him, he'd never have made it, whoever he is.'

She didn't reply.

'So he'll have something to thank you for.'

'Please,' she begged, 'can't you go faster?'

Jeff said, 'We won't take long.'

She levelled the glasses again, but the shaking of the car made it impossible to see or focus properly. She put them down. The man on the hillside seemed to be moving helplessly, without reason or design. A step here, a step there, he floundered as if he could not see where he was going. He was tall—*Nigel was tall*. Of course it was Nigel; fate wouldn't be so cruel as to deny that now.

'Look!' exclaimed Jeff.

The man above seemed to break into a run, as if he had seen them, but after three or four steps he collapsed. Sight of that seemed to cut through Della like a knife.

'He's down,' Jeff said. He would always labour the obvious, but Della did not notice that now. All she wanted was to reach the fallen man.

He lay still, his hat dislodged, his hair burnished by the fierce sun. He was fair-haired, *and Nigel was fair-haired.*

Della saw Jeff staring at her, as if he, too, had realised that it might indeed be Nigel. He didn't speak. They were only a hundred yards away, moving so slowly that it would be quicker to go on by foot. Della opened the door. Hot, dust-laden air swept in. Jeff made no attempt to stop her as the car slowed down.

'Careful!' he called.

She nearly pitched forward, recovered, waited until the car was at a standstill, and jumped. Although pain shot through her bruised knee and made her stagger, she did not stop but half ran towards the man who lay so still.

At last she could see his face, a gaunt skeleton of a face, jaw thrusting against the bone, eyes buried, cheeks so sunken that it was almost like a death's-head. All that was bad; all that was horrible, but the worst thing of all was that she could not be sure whether this man was Nigel.

She stood staring down, unbelieving because she could not tell. This man's face was so thin, so like a death's head.

Jeff reached her side.

'Poor devil,' he said. 'Poor bloody devil.' He went on one knee, feeling for the man's pulse. 'He's alive, anyway. Just.' He slid one arm under the man's waist and another under his shoulder and lifted him as if he weighed no more than a child. 'Open the back door, Della.'

She stared at the skeleton face, at skin grey and dry as

parchment, and then turned away, choking back sobs. She could not tell if it were Nigel. It was almost worse than being sure that it was not. All this time and she did not recognise him.

She opened the door and stood aside.

'Cushions,' Jeff said brusquely.

He kept the cushions in the luggage compartment. She ran round and opened it, took out two cushions, and placed them on the back seat. Carefully, as if handling some precious thing, Jeff put the man down on them. The pitiful wasted body seemed to crumple up. The kneecaps seemed huge against skinny legs; she could see halfway up his thighs, and the leg there was no thicker than her arm.

'Just moisten his lips,' Jeff said. It was an order.

Della went round to the front of the car, unhooked the canvas water bottle from the radiator cap, and returned to the car. She unscrewed the cap quite steadily; she felt better now that she had something to do. She spilled only a little water as she poured it into a tin mug on the back window ledge. Jeff always had things ready, was never unprepared. Sometimes she thought of him as the biggest and best Boy Scout she had ever met.

She dipped the corner of her handkerchief into the water and ran it over the unconscious man's lips, eyes, and forehead. He did not stir. His eyelids were thin and blue-veined and stretched like a skin over his eyes.

Could this be Nigel?

His skin was so dry, his lips pitifully bruised and cracked. There had never been a blemish on his face, no mark by which she could identify him. As she dipped her finger into the water, allowing the drops to fall into the closed lips, and watching it seeping through into his mouth, the awful irony of the situation made her feel sick.

The car began to move slowly.

She sat on one side of this near-dead man, who was nothing but skin and bone, without any certain knowledge that he was or was not Nigel. She tried to reason with herself, to prepare herself against finding that he was a stranger. Everyone who came from the west came over that hill; there was a deep ravine which prevented them coming any other way. The odds against this being Nigel were overwhelming. For once she was able to put herself in Jeff's position, to see how improbable it was that this should be Nigel, to realise how absurd her vigil must seem to everyone else.

Jeff asked, over his shoulder, 'How is he?'

'The same.'

'Taking any water?'

'Not really.'

'Just cool him down a bit,' Jeff advised. 'We won't be long. He'll pull through. I've seen them worse than he is, and they've pulled through.'

He didn't ask Della if she was now convinced that it wasn't Nigel. He took it for granted that it wasn't, of course.

There was one way of telling, only one. Hunger and thirst could reduce a man to skin and bone but could not remove a birthmark. There was one, the size of a hen's egg, on Nigel's thigh, it was just below the hipbone, a little towards the front. Unless he was naked she could not tell. She wanted so desperately to know.

The khaki shorts were torn and bleached by the sun to no colour at all. Once they had been snug; now they were tied round at the wasted waist with a piece of palm frond made into rope. The knot was very tight.

'We'll take him to Ma Parkin,' Jeff said.

It was the obvious place to take a stranger. But Nigel . . .

'You hear?'

They were nearing the first house now. Mrs. Cratton was still swinging to and fro, to and fro, in the old wicker chair. She waved and called out. It was only five minutes more to the Parkins' place.

Della said in a low-pitched voice, 'I must know.'

Jeff heard it.

'What's that?'

'Nothing,' she said. 'Nothing.' Then she thrust up the roughly made rope and pulled down the shorts. She had not really expected to see the birthmark, had steeled herself to accept disappointment.

But there it was!

She saw that birthmark and knew beyond all doubt that Nigel had come back.

She sat quite still, aware of a new kind of quiet within her. It was a strange, eerie feeling. There was a sense of exultation, too. She watched the road in front of her. It ran straight on to the Parkins' place, but her house—their house—was along on the left, past the tiny graveyard with its five stone crosses and its many crosses of wood and the shapeless mounds which marked the other graves.

'Go to my place, Jeff,' she said.

He turned his thick neck and protested, 'No. Della, don't fool yourself.'

'*My* place!'

'You can't look after him like Ma Parkin.'

'I can look after my own husband,' Della said.

'Della, stop fooling yourself!' Jeff turned so sharply that he stalled the engine. 'There's no way you can—'

'There is a way,' she insisted. 'This is my husband.'

She thought Jeff would say that he did not believe her, thought he would try to persuade her to change her mind. He did not.

Perhaps the calmness of her expression influenced him. There was a puzzled look in his eyes as he glanced at Nigel and then back at her. At last he turned to the wheel.

She looked down at Nigel, who had come home.

It was like looking upon the face of a stranger.

She did not need any help to put Nigel to bed. She sponged his body carefully, gently, and now and again she thought of the body which had been. It was hard to believe that he would ever again be strong, with firm white flesh covering these sharp bones which themselves seemed to have wasted away. Wrinkled, browny grey, lifeless—it was like sponging a corpse.

She drew a sheet up over him, then lowered the Venetian blind so that the room was in semi-darkness. She went to the old tattered, stained pair of shorts, the bush jacket which was so worn that it was difficult to understand how it hung together, the battered hat, the 'belt' of palm-frond rope. She drew this through her fingers, feeling the knobbly pieces of the palm; it was made by someone inexperienced, was nothing like a Bantu would make. Had he made it himself?

Footsteps outside made her look up. A shadow passed the room, big and dark; Ma's. She went to the living room as Ma tapped on the door. Ma Parkin believed in conceding as well as demanding privacy.

'Come in,' Della called.

The door creaked open. A huge woman dressed in a soiled white smock came in laboriously. She looked around, then approached Della.

'So it was all worth it, Della.'

'It was worth it,' Della said.

'You won't mind me being frank?' The little mouth in the full, pale face seemed to move like that of a ventriloquist's doll. The big, surprisingly big, and beautiful doe-like eyes were filled with concern.

'Ma, it's Nigel.'

'Can you be positive, Della?'

'Yes.'

'You've wanted him back so bad, maybe you're just telling yourself this is your man.'

'Ma, he's Nigel.'

'How can you be sure?'

Della turned to the bedroom, and the big woman followed her; her movements were more waddle than walk. Della went straight to the bed and pulled back the sheet. The birthmark showed up starkly, for she had drawn a pair of jockey pants over Nigel's legs and round his body. They were loose about him, but the plain white showed up the reddish colour of the egg-shaped mark.

Ma Parkin stared at it, then looked at Della and smiled very slowly.

'I couldn't be more pleased for my own daughter,' she declared. 'You certainly have been rewarded, Della. You certainly have. And when he comes round he'll see you've kept this place like a palace for him. Just like a palace!' She paused. 'You know you must get some nourishment into him, don't you? I've brought some chicken broth and some Bovril. And he's got to have saline injections. I've brought everything. I've had a lot of experience in this kind of thing, Della. You won't mind if I help, will you?'

'I'll be grateful,' Della said. 'Very grateful.'

'The first thing I'd do is burn those filthy old clothes,' Ma Parkin said soon afterwards.

Della didn't speak but did not burn the bush shirt or the shorts. With half of her mind she thought, 'Some old boy can find a use for them.' With the other half she thought much less positively that they would keep her close to the past.

During the next three days Nigel lay like a corpse, with no noticeable change except perhaps in colour; his cheeks became a little less like a parchment. Not once did his eyes open, and not once did he move. Della forced chicken soup and Bovril between his lips, and the muscles of his neck moved to show that he was swallowing, but that was all. Night and morning Ma Parkin came over to give him an injection which Della herself could have given just as well, but it would have been unkind to the older woman to insist. Jeff came each day but said very little.

Della felt quite calm, but there was a sense of unreality all the time.

The remarkable thing was that Nigel still seemed a stranger, as he had when she had first been certain who he was. It was as if the years of waiting had been their own reward and his return a strange anticlimax. She felt no emotion, no sting of tears. She tended for him as if he were precious, none the less, watching for the first indication that he was coming out of his coma. If he didn't respond to Ma Parkin's treatment and her own very soon, she would have to send for a doctor from Buckingham, seventy miles away. But she felt almost as sure that he would come round as she had felt sure he would return.

The strangest thing was sleeping in the same room.

She slept next to him on a camp bed, within hand's reach. In fact she mostly dozed, half expecting him to stir during the night, or to hear him try to call out. On the fourth night, when there was still no change, she slept more heavily.

At first there was no sound to disturb her; there was just the night's silence. Then a noise, very faint and far away, came into the room. She did not hear it.

The noise grew louder and took on identifiable form the sound of footsteps.

She slept on.

The footsteps drew near the foot of the three steps which led to the stoep and the front door. There was a creak of boards, then a fainter creak as the door began to open.

Still she did not hear.

The door of the bedroom opened. The room was very dark and no glimmer of light showed. A man stood there, breathing very softly. Della did not stir. The man could just discern the camp bed, the white sheet, the white pillow, and Della's dark head. He drew closer. He stepped past the head of the bed and stood above Nigel. He took something out of his pocket—a scarf, folded over and over. He lowered this towards Nigel's face, every movement slow and stealthy, until it covered Nigel's nose and mouth.

The man began to press on it, so as to prevent Nigel from taking in his pitiful little breaths.

Della became aware of vague sounds, of something different. She lay on the narrow bed, fully awake on the instant. Had Nigel called out? Had he stirred? She looked towards him, saw something dark across his face and a hand above it, pressing. She could not see anything else because the man was standing behind her.

She cried out, 'What are you doing?'

The man snatched his hand away. Della tried to sit up, but before she could a hand clamped about her neck, the fingers tightening, fierce and hard. She could hardly breathe. She writhed and struggled and struck at the strong forearm, but it made no difference. He was choking her. Her breast was heaving; strange misty lights flickered in front of her eyes. She felt the strength ebbing out of her as if it were life itself.

CHAPTER III

THE INTRUDER

'How much do you say they were worth?' inquired Patrick Dawlish quietly.

He was by nature a polite man, although large, and by nature found it easy to be incredulous. This did not show in his cornflower-blue eyes as he stared at Colonel Van Diesek, of the Pretoria Police Force. Although Van Diesek had flown here from South Africa, and although he doubtless meant what he said, Dawlish was far from convinced that he had the figures right.

'Two hundred million rands,' Van Diesek repeated.

'Ah,' said Dawlish. 'One hundred million pounds.'

'Your arithmetic is very good,' the South African said dryly. 'Major Dawlish, you do not believe me, do you?'

'I think there might be some margin of error,' Dawlish murmured.

'There is no error,' Van Diesek assured him. His voice was harsher; his manner showed the beginning of annoyance. He was a tall, big, strong-featured man with pale-grey eyes, cropped hair. He had a military bearing even when he sat opposite

Dawlish in the big room at New Scotland Yard. The room over-looked the Embankment and the Thames. It was bright and sunny but cool with the breeze coming in at two open windows. The tops of the plane trees, a pale green, waved just outside the window. 'The diamonds have been stolen in large and small quantities over many years. I have been in charge of the inves-tigations, and while I have had some small successes, in the main I have failed and failed terribly. There are eleven major and many smaller diamond mines in South Africa, and over the years each has been robbed, sometimes of very great quantities.'

'Have we heard about this here?' asked Dawlish interestedly.

'The thefts have been internal matters. We have from time to time notified you and Interpol of thefts and asked your members to look out for marked uncut stones but have never notified you of the quantities involved. It has been to avoid publicity. The main distributing agency, United Diamond Distributors, has been most anxious to make sure that nothing happened to disturb the market. So small thefts have been reported, but not the large ones; the total value is beyond dispute. The conse-quences of the cumulative loss can be very serious.'

'To whom in particular?' asked Dawlish.

'To the diamond industry in my country and so to its economy,' Van Diesek declared. His manner was a curious mixture of aggression and pleading. 'As the U.D.D. makes clear, "The loss is sufficient to affect the price of diamonds if released upon the world market." Do you find difficulty in believing that?'

Dawlish's eyes crinkled at the corners.

'Yes, of course, but obviously a hundred million pounds' worth would do that.'

'You doubtless know, how many people do not know, that the price of diamonds is controlled by the producing companies,' went on the South African. 'There is some loss by stealing, some by smuggling, always a danger of a falling market because individual mines might wish to raise money and flood the market with stones at a low price. The I.D.B.—illicit diamond buyers— are always active, but on a limited scale. It would not serve their purpose to place any large quantity of diamonds on the market at one time, because it would bring the price of the stones too low. I have worked ceaselessly on the investigation and have come to the conclusion that the diamonds have not been sold in any great quantities but are being released very slowly, so as to hold up the market value. It follows that if such a large number has been stolen and few sold, there is somewhere a very big hoard of the diamonds. In fact, this is my conviction. My fear—and that of United Diamond Distributors—is that they will indeed be released on to the world markets suddenly and will so flood them that prices will fall very low.'

'The bottom could be knocked out of the market, in other words,' Dawlish said.

'Exactly, Major. It is essential to find those missing diamonds, Major Dawlish, absolutely essential. They must not be allowed to flood the market.' Vehemence made the hard voice even harsher. 'It is certain you can assist.'

'If I can, I certainly will,' said Dawlish. He felt formal and even a little pompous and could understand if he was getting under Van Diesek's skin. 'Over how long a period have they been missing, do you say?'

'We have been aware of the situation for four years but became seriously alarmed when a particularly large loss occurred last month.'

'How large?' inquired Dawlish.

'Two million pounds' worth were taken from an underground store in Kimberley.'

'And you've kept such a fabulous loss a secret?'

'Of course. It would be a bad thing if the newspapers were to know.'

'Why?' asked Dawlish. 'Publicity might worry the thieves.'

'Worry might also alarm them into selling quickly and so put too many diamonds on the market,' Van Diesek insisted. 'Mr. Dawlish, you have much more influence with the Conference than I. I ask you please to use that influence. You have there a file giving all the details. Once you have studied it I am sure you will agree on the gravity of the case. This will not only affect South Africa. It will affect the world. I have no doubt it is a case for the Conference.'

'Yes,' said Dawlish. 'Certainly I think it is.' He saw the South African's eyes light up. 'There is a Conference session tomorrow, here in London. I'll be glad to raise this matter.' After a pause he went on: 'Will you come to present the case as it is an international, not simply a national emergency?'

'If you give me the opportunity I will be very grateful,' Van Diesek said. 'So will my superiors. One thing, Major Dawlish. Will there be any newspapermen present?'

'None at all,' Dawlish assured him. 'Until you agree that publicity will help, none at all.'

Van Diesek stood up, bowed formally from the waist, and shook hands. The pressure of his grip told Dawlish just how much this decision mattered to him. Dawlish was already aware of some of the problems. Having borders with Southern Rhodesia, West Africa, and Portuguese East Africa, South Africa was particularly vulnerable to the smuggling of gold and diamonds, two of her most vital commodities. Without co-operation from the police of all three countries it would be difficult, probably impossible, to trace the thieves. And two hundred million rands was a fantastic sum—enough in itself to demand probing questions. Why keep the truth of such losses from the world? Why wait until they had become so enormous before asking for outside help? Why allow so long a time to pass?

There might be political answer to the questions; there might be rational answers too. The big diamond combines were a law unto themselves. But the questions needed asking—and answering. Some answers might be in Van Diesek's report.

Dawlish leaned towards a shelf near him, took down a Philips World Atlas, and thumbed through it until he found a map of southern Africa. Yes, the proximity was dangerous, and South Africa might find difficulty in getting the co-operation she needed from each one of the neighbouring countries. The Crime Conference could get such co-operation, for the Conference— known popularly as the Crime Haters—had an organisation already set up, with liaison officers from each major country active within itself.

If that vast fortune in diamonds had been stolen, if it was to be used to flood the market, then only the Crime Haters could possibly handle the investigation.

He closed the atlas and began to study the file which Van Diesek had left. It was much more than a report on the latest loss of an enormous store of diamonds from the vaults of a 'small' mine near Kimberley. It was the story of the unending war between the diamond companies in the ring, which held diamond prices by means of organised scarcity, and thieves and smugglers. Dawlish, who had a nodding acquaintance with the history of diamonds in South Africa, was at once appalled and enthralled.

He could hardly wait for Van Diesek to present his case to the Conference tomorrow.

Van Diesek left New Scotland Yard in a much happier frame of mind than he had entered it. First and last a policeman, he was unavoidably affected by politics, and there was too often a clash of interests between South Africa and other nations. He had often worked with the Yard and the police of other nations, however, and always found the police themselves objective. There was an identity of outlook among policemen which overcame most barriers and most prejudices. In the past, however, he had never needed co-operation on so big an issue as this. He had not felt sure that he would get it, and as he went down the steps of the big building, he was smiling to himself. He should have known better than to have doubted Dawlish. Many peculiar stories circulated about Dawlish, who was known to be very much the Englishman. He had worked for the British Intelligence Service during the war. He had fought in some of the most savage actions in that same war. He had been parachuted into Occupied France and other parts of Europe. He had become famous and notorious, according to one's point of view. He was an international name among police long before he had been appointed Deputy Commissioner of Police at New Scotland Yard.

The appointment was for one special reason: his knowledge of international crime and his acquaintance with policemen all over the world.

Van Diesek pictured Dawlish's huge frame as he had stood up behind his desk and could almost feel the pressure of his strong fingers.

He smiled more happily.

With Dawlish and the Crime Haters active, there was a good chance that the mystery of the stolen diamonds would be solved, and if it was, it would be the high light as well as the culmination of his career. No one in South Africa, probably no one in the world, had such an exhaustive knowledge of diamond stealing and smuggling. He was the liaison between the police and the diamond companies and had been so for many years—long before the Union became the Republic. He was quite sure in his mind that in recent years the illicit diamond buyers had become better and more skilfully organised than ever before. Time and time again he had wanted to consult the Crime Conference, but until now had not had sufficient to go on, and his own superiors had vetoed the approach.

Now he had his way.

He crossed the Embankment, with his brief case tucked underneath his arm. For ten minutes he walked towards Blackfriars, taking in all the bustling activity of the river, the gaily coloured pleasure boats on the October afternoon, the barges, the small launches. At Cleopatra's Needle he stopped and turned back.

A man only a few yards behind him, stopped in his tracks. Van Diesek had seen him before—at the airport that morning. But for his preoccupation with what had happened with Dawlish he would have noticed him before this. He evaded the man, nodded an apology for almost bumping into him, then stepped to the kerb. Almost at once a taxi came along, plying for hire; that was the good thing about London. He waved it to stop.

'Linden Hotel, please.'

'Right.' The driver pulled down the hire sign to start his meter ticking. Van Diesek sat in a corner and looked out of the rear window. He saw the man he had recognised at the kerb, waving to a taxi which passed him.

Van Diesek settled back comfortably and wondered how best to deal with this situation. A word with Dawlish would be the best thing; he himself could do nothing about the man here, but if he lodged a complaint the London police could act. This man's arrest could lead to important discoveries; the essential thing was to make sure that he was not alarmed. Van Diesek paid off his taxi outside the Linden Hotel, which was near Welbeck Street, just behind Oxford Street. He went into the old-fashioned red-plush and dark-oak furnished hall. The porter on duty smiled.

'Nice day, sir.'

'A very good day.' Van Diesek went into the tea lounge, which had a window overlooking the street. An elderly waitress came up, dressed in black with a small white apron.

'No tea, thank you.'

'Very good, sir.'

A taxi drew up a few doors along. Van Diesek stood by the side of the curtained window, looking out. The man from the taxi approached; it was the man from the Embankment.

'I've got him,' Van Diesek said to himself in Afrikaans. The waitress looked at him inquiringly. He went briskly into the hall and to the old lift. A small boy operated it.

'Floor, sir?'

'Five.'

'Five it is, sir.'

Van Diesek was not interested in a mildly cheeky boy, only in getting to the telephone in his room and calling Dawlish. There was every reason to believe that the man in Linden Square would wait until he left the hotel again, but nevertheless the South African policeman felt a driving sense of urgency. It was almost as if he realised that he had little time left.

He walked along the squeaky corridor, taking his key out of his pocket. He did not give a thought to the possibility that anyone might be inside the room. Even when he opened the door, there was nothing further from his mind.

He stepped inside, pushing the door to behind him—and then stopped short.

A man was at the chest of drawers on the other side of the

bed. On this bed was Van Diesek's suitcase—his only piece of luggage. The man was staring at him. He had one hand in his pocket.

In Afrikaans, Van Diesek said. 'So I have no further to look.'

The other man stood absolutely still. He was tall and thin, with sharp features and a pointed chin. His hair was a gingery colour. His right hand did not move from his pocket.

'Your friend outside didn't have time to warn you,' Van Diesek said. For the second time that day he felt a great sense of elation; it was hard to believe that he could have such luck as this.

The telephone began to ring.

'There he is,' Van Diesek gibed. 'Answer him.'

The telephone sounded loud and harsh. The instrument was by the side of the bed, nearer Van Diesek than the man. It kept on ringing.

'Then I will answer it for you.' The policeman from Pretoria took a short step towards the instrument. 'And don't try to stop me.'

The thin man took his hand from his pocket. He held a small snub-nosed automatic. There was no change in his expression but a great one in Van Diesek's, who paused in the middle of his step and said gruffly: 'Put that down. You are no murderer.' The ringing sound was very harsh.

The man raised the gun and pointed it. There was a look of absolute disbelief in Van Diesek's eyes, yet a look of horror too. He made a desperate leap to one side, but he had no room to manoeuvre. He saw the other's finger squeeze the trigger and felt the tremendous blow of a bullet on his temple.

He died on that instant.

The man who had killed him slid the gun into his pocket as he moved round the foot of the bed. He bent over Van Diesek's crumpled body, and his heel touched—only just touched—the blood which was spilling on to the carpet. The bell was still ringing. He bent down and picked up Van Diesek's brief case, tucked it under his arm, and stepped to the door.

The ringing stopped.

The murderer listened for fully a minute but heard no sound He stepped outside and closed the door quietly. He went to the stairway at one side of the lift, pulled his hat over his eyes, and began to walk down.

He met no one.

He stepped across the little red-plush entrance hall. The porter was at the desk with a man and woman who were registering, and no one appeared to notice the killer. He went outside. He saw the man who had followed Van Diesek on the other side of the road near a telephone kiosk. They did not acknowledge each other. The murderer turned the corner into Wigmore Street and saw two taxis for hire. He stopped the first one.

'London Airport,' he ordered, and settled back comfortably in the taxi—just as Van Diesek had done only half an hour before. Then he opened the stolen brief case, smiling in anticipation of what he was going to find. He took out the papers and began to look through them. Slowly his smile faded and a hard, bleak look replaced it.

CHAPTER IV

THE REPORT

About the time that Van Diesek's murderer was looking through the stolen brief case, Patrick Dawlish was placing a large forefinger on a bell push by his side. Almost at once one of the two doors leading into the office opened and a man appeared. He wore clerical grey. He was pale and very slightly plump. Behind horn-rimmed glasses his eyes seemed large and too pale.

Dawlish picked up the South African report and thumbed the pages as an expert might thumb a pack of cards. The noise—*whirr!*—seemed very loud in the office.

'Forty-seven pages,' he announced. 'Single spacing.'

The other man frowned, creating a deep groove between his eyes.

'That is a little over eight hours' work. Say six pages an hour—may I keep two typists late tonight?'

'Permission to pay overtime granted,' said Dawlish. He grinned as he handed the report over. He had an attractive expression when he grinned, and it gave him a quality difficult to define. Perhaps it emphasised the fact that but for his broken nose he would have been strikingly handsome for such a giant. 'Are you going to be one of the typists?'

'I would gladly, but there is too much preparation for the Conference meeting in the morning. I listened with great interest to your conversation with Colonel Van Diesek.'

'I'll bet you did!'

'May I make a suggestion?'

'I wouldn't know how to stop you.'

The man in dark grey ignored the sarcasm.

'If you yourself presented the facts to the Conference, I think it would be much more effective. Colonel Van Diesek's manner might appear somewhat overbearing because of over-emphasis.'

'He feels too much for his case,' Dawlish said. 'I'll think about it.'

'Thank you. How many copies of the report will you need?'

'One for each member, the usual for the secretariat, and a dozen or so spares. Once it's circulated we will have a devil of a job to keep it from the press, and when we have to come across we might as well have a few copies handy.'

'I'll see to it.'

'Thanks, Temple.'

'One other thing, sir. Mrs. Dawlish telephoned and I promised you would call her back when you were free.'

'I'll call her at once,' Dawlish promised.

He tried, but the number of his flat was engaged. He went to the window and looked across the Thames towards a tall building just in sight beyond the Houses of Parliament. The sun reflected on the window of his penthouse flat, where Felicity was probably sitting on the arm of a chair talking gaily into the telephone. Nearly everything Felicity did when she was free from anxiety was gay; perhaps vivacious was a better word. Dawlish was smiling as he thought of her. They had been married over twenty years ago, and life together was still very, very good.

He went back to his private telephone and dialled the number again. It was still engaged. She was having quite a time!

He wondered why she had telephoned him.

Then another telephone bell rang. It was Van Woelden, the Netherlands delegate to the Conference tomorrow, calling from The Hague. Dawlish talked briskly for ten minutes, and as soon as he rang off the buzzer of a third telephone sounded, and its light glowed. This was also from overseas.

'Mr. Sobimoto of Tokyo is calling, sir,' Temple said.

'I'll talk to him,' Dawlish said.

Sobimoto, the Japanese delegate to the Conference, was extremely apologetic. There were some problems in Tokyo which had made it impossible to get away, so he would not have the pleasure of meeting Major Dawlish again tomorrow and was extremely sorry. He had been particularly anxious to pay his respects when Major Dawlish was in the chair at the Conference. Dawlish did nothing to cut him short; the odd thing about the Japanese was that although their courtesies often seemed insincere, they were extremely important to them.

At last Sobimoto finished. Almost at once Temple came in with the provisional agenda for the Conference meeting. Dawlish thought of calling Felicity, decided not to, changed his mind, and found the engaged signal still buzzing.

He frowned.

'She's having a really long natter,' he remarked, and rang for Temple. 'Try my home number every five minutes or so, will you?'

'Yes, sir.'

Dawlish picked up the agenda and soon forgot Felicity. There was no reason why he should not, no reason at all why he should think she was in any danger. The agenda demanded all his attention.

The Conference met frequently, under different chairmen from time to time. Most countries in the world were represented at its sessions by their top policemen. It was in a way like Interpol but had more authority in its own right; in fact, it was the embyro of a truly international police force, working on much the same lines as an Allied Secret Service had worked during the war. It had developed very quickly since it had started four years earlier. Dawlish had been Britain's representative since then. This was his first meeting in the chair, and he was looking forward to it more than he admitted to anyone except his wife.

Tomorrow and on each of the next three days these men from all over the world would discuss world problems in crime. The criminal was becoming more and more international. Frontiers were easy to cross by air; time was no longer a hazardous factor in disposing of stolen jewels or in escaping from one country to another. As the countries of the world drew closer and the economic and political problems of one affected those of another, so did police affairs.

Very few people even suspected the fervour and conviction Dawlish felt for the international policemen's organisation—a crime detection and prevention force quite distinct from the 'policing' carried out by the United Nations.

He made a few alterations to the agenda, putting Van Diesek's problem high on the list so as to make sure that there was good time for it to be discussed tomorrow. Temple was probably right about the South African's overbearing manner, but the other policemen would be quick to see the burning sincerity of the man.

Dawlish looked at Big Ben, just in sight if he leaned forward.

'Half-past five!' he exclaimed. And a moment later: 'I wonder where Fel's nipped off to.'

He took it for granted that his wife had telephoned earlier to say that she was going out. Then, with his police-trained mind, he wondered why she would have asked him to call back had she been going out.

It still did not occur to him that there might be the slightest need for fear for Felicity.

Earlier in the afternoon, when Felicity had telephoned the Yard, she had not thought of fear.

She had had a letter by the second post, an invitation for them both to a country house party that weekend; some friends were expecting friends from America. If the Conference ended in time, Pat would love to go.

'I'll ask him to call you as soon as he is free,' Temple promised.

Felicity rang off, went closer to the window, and looked across at the red brick of New Scotland Yard. She could just see Pat's window. From this spot high above most buildings in the heart of London there was a magnificent panoramic view, with the Houses of Parliament in the foreground, and Westminster Abbey just in sight at one side. St. Paul's was far off, with the bridges, the fine new buildings, the fine old buildings, the shimmering Thames making its lazy curving and shimmering way in the sun.

'Beautiful,' Felicity said. 'Quite beautiful.'

She said that at least once on every sunny day.

There was a ring at the front door.

She was alone in the flat; she nearly always was in the afternoons. She wasn't expecting anyone and did not trouble to speculate on whom the caller might be, just glanced into a mirror, tidied her hair with her hands, and opened the front door.

A man stood there, a stranger. She took an instant dislike to him. His features were so thin and sharp that he had almost a hatchet face. He had very bright, greeny eyes.

'Good afternoon.'

'Good afternoon.' He had some kind of accent which she could not place. 'Is Major Dawlish in please?'

'I'm not expecting him until about six o'clock,' said Felicity. 'If it is urgent, you can find him at Scotland Yard.'

'Are you sure that he's there?' There was something aggressive in this man's manner, and she did not like him at all.

'Yes. He's in conference.'

'Are you Mrs. Dawlish?'

'Yes.'

'May I telephone your husband?' the man asked, and took a step forward.

Instinctively she felt she could not trust him. There was something in his manner and his expression she disliked very much.

'There is a telephone downstairs in the hall . . .' she began.

Alarm flared up in her as he lunged forward and thrust out his hands, pushing her. She missed a step and went stumbling backward. The stranger stepped swiftly after her and closed the door. Even in that moment of panic she noticed that he closed the door quietly. She recovered her balance and made a futile attempt to snatch up an ash tray, to throw at him. The shiny glass slipped out of her fingers and bumped painfully against her leg as it fell. The man moved very fast. She struck out at him with her right hand, but instead of striking it aside, he caught her wrist and twisted.

She gasped in pain.

He twisted again and swung her round. Pain shot up her arm to her shoulder. Her back was towards him now, and her arm was thrust up behind her, so that she could not move. She was facing the mirror in which she had just tidied her hair. He was standing close behind her, his face looming above her left shoulder.

He seemed to sneer at her.

'Does that hurt?'

He gave her arm a jolt. She winced.

'I asked you if that hurt.'

'You know it hurts!'

'Just you remember it can hurt a lot more if you don't do what I tell you.'

Felicity didn't speak. She knew just how right he was and needed no telling that he was utterly ruthless. She hadn't the faintest idea what he wanted. He was strong enough to make her do whatever he wished. Oh, God! He could do anything with her. She did not even know for certain that he wanted Pat; he might have come simply for her.

Why?

He slackened his grip slightly, easing a little of the strain, then slid his free hand over her shoulder, under her blouse. She hated the touch of his hand on her skin. If he went further, how could she stop him? She stared at his reflection in the mirror, forcing herself to show defiance, fighting against the compulsion to show her dread.

She thought with a kind of cold desperation; 'If I back-heel I might make him let go, but what can I do after that?'

His hand stopped, fingers at the beginning of the swell of her breast. He was grinning, showing narrow, shiny teeth. It was almost as if he were gloating over her.

What did he want?

'If you do what I tell you, you won't get hurt,' he said.

She had no idea whether she could believe him.

'Understand that?'

'I heard you,' she managed to say.

'You won't get hurt if you do what I tell you, but you'll get hurt badly if you make any difficulties. Understand that?'

She made herself answer yes. She still had no idea what he wanted, why he was so insistent that she should do what he ordered. What kind of thing would it be?

'I'm going to let you go,' he said. 'Just walk straight to your bedroom.'

She caught her breath.

He did not speak again but let her go, the touch of his fingers lingering. He watched her intently in the mirror as he did so, and she thought he expected her to put up a fight. It was almost as if he wanted her to.

She did not kick back or move or jump forward. She must judge the perfection of the moment for any such attempt. She might not get more than one chance; she might not get a chance at all.

'Get a move on,' he ordered.

She turned to the door leading to the little hallway. The bedroom door, beyond it, stood ajar. She shivered. She went slowly, desperately anxious to outwit him. If she ran into the bedroom and slammed the door, could she hold it fast against him? Would anyone hear if she shouted? There was one other flat up here, but the tenants were on holiday.

She pushed open the door.

He gripped her shoulder tightly, painfully.

'Go in and lie on the bed, face downward,' he said. 'And don't kick or scream. I'm going to tie you to the bed so that you can't do any harm and can't warn your husband.

Again Felicity caught her breath, and a new fear added to that which already filled her, a greater fear for Pat.

'He's got something I need badly,' the man said. 'He'll bring it here to do some homework. If he doesn't have it he can't do it, can he? He'll have to pay more attention to you.'

She jumped forward into the room and tried to slam the

door, but the man got his foot in the way. She thrust all her strength against it, but he forced it open. The rage in his eyes terrified her. He jumped at her, brushed aside her hands, and gripped her neck.

He began to squeeze, his fingers tightening. She kicked and struggled but all in vain. Misty lights swam in front of her eyes and she felt the strength ebbing out of her whole being.

CHAPTER V

KISS

Dawlish stepped out of the lift at the top of the building and crossed to the staircase which led up to the penthouses. He had no thought of any kind of trouble, was simply wondering whether Felicity would be home. This was a case he would enjoy discussing with her, and few things gave her more pleasure than full and free talk with him over a case. That was some compensation for the long hours, sometimes weeks, which she spent alone while he was working or out of the country. Anything to do with diamonds would interest her particularly.

One hundred million pounds' worth!

Felicity simply wouldn't believe it.

Dawlish sobered. No one could really take in such figures. The more he studied and thought about the case, the more it fascinated him.

His keys clinked as he took them out of his trousers pocket and selected the front door one. As he turned it, he hoped Felicity would be in. A kiss, a drink, a little teasing, and supper in the kitchen while they talked.

He heard nothing. Had Felicity been home she would have

heard him open the door and would have called out by now. Pity. Perhaps she wouldn't be long.

His telephone bell rang.

It was not the telephone, and was not the silence before it, but a curious little *cluck* of sound which put him on the alert. The main telephone was in the drawing room, but there was an extension in the bedroom. The extension bell was ringing. He could answer the call from either place but was a foot or two nearer the bedroom than the living room. He turned towards it and went across.

He heard another slight sound.

Possibly Felicity was playing some joke on him, but he did not really think she would play this way. The sound was now behind him, at the living-room door. He did not glance round but turned the handle of the bedroom door, at his most sensitive state of alertness. Years of training had given him what amounted to a sixth sense; trifles which were unfamiliar or struck a false note took on a deep significance. He had learned one invaluable lesson for such times: never do the expected. Now he was quite sure there was someone in the living-room doorway, but whoever it was did not know that he realised it.

So—what was the least expected thing to do?

He turned the handle and pushed the door; it was locked.

Felicity never locked herself in, there was no reason at all why she should. This door had been locked from the outside. He stood back, apparently in bewilderment. The bell kept on ringing; it had been going on for a long time. He had no idea what he would see if he turned round, but he did know that whoever was there would expect him to turn at any moment.

He gripped the handle of the door.

'Fel!' he cried. 'Are you in there?'

Only the telephone answered.

He drew back, paused, then hurled his two hundred and fifty pounds at the door. He had the knack of breaking down a door and knew exactly where to put on the pressure. The door creaked and groaned. He crashed against it again and as he did so looked over his shoulder.

A sharp-faced man with a gun in his hand was halfway across the little hall. The assault on the door had taken him completely by surprise, and in that moment of indecision he was vulnerable.

Dawlish hurled his brief case at him. The man dodged and squeezed the trigger; there was a sharp report of a shot, but the bullet hit the floor. Before the man could shoot again, Dawlish reached and struck him two savage blows with the palm of his great hand. The sharp thwacking sound was like the crack of whips. The man staggered sideways, missed his footing, and fell. Dawlish strode across and kicked the automatic away as it hit the floor. Then he turned and rammed the door again.

Felicity lay face downward, spread-eagled on the big double bed. A sheet tied her ankles to the foot of the bed, which had an intricately carved panel. Rope round each wrist tied her to the top corners. Her face was turned towards him. Her eyes were closed, and she lay absolutely still, as if nothing would ever disturb her again.

Adhesive plaster covered her mouth and pushed up against her nose.

She looked like death.

He heard a sound behind him, glanced round and saw the man on his feet again. He had his, Dawlish's, brief case under his arm and was moving towards the front door. When he saw Dawlish he put on a spurt.

That moment was one of the longest in Dawlish's life. He had to make a decision in itself, awful in its possible consequences. Minutes might make all the difference to his wife, could conceivably make the difference between life and death. He ought to go to her without wasting even a split second. Yet he was a policeman, and the man heading for the door was a dangerous criminal; he had come here and attacked Felicity with this vicious violence, and only a hardened criminal would have come and behaved like that.

There was no time to think, only to make the decision, and it seemed to Dawlish that all the possibilities went through his mind as he made it.

He jumped forward. The man slammed the door. Dawlish stopped it from closing and reached the landing a yard behind the intruder, who ran towards the head of the stairs. Dawlish stretched out his right leg and kicked the man in the back of the foot. The man pitched down the stairs, with Dawlish after him. He fell in a heap at the foot of the stairs with his head twisted round. There was terror in his eyes, terror caused by the expression on Dawlish's face.

Dawlish bent down, yanked him to his feet, and hit him, once. There was a sharp crack of sound. Dawlish stopped him from falling, gripped the back of his coat, and dragged him upstairs. He knew from the dead weight the limpness of the body that the man was unconscious.

Dawlish dragged him into the room, dropped him, and ran into the bedroom. Felicity had not stirred.

'Fel,' he said in a choky voice. 'Fel.'

He picked at the corner of the adhesive tape, without hesitating for a fraction of a second, and wrenched it off. Two or three pin-point globules of blood appeared almost at once on Felicity's lips, and a patch of skin tore off a corner of one. Because of the pressure her mouth looked bloodless; her face did too.

Like death.

The telephone rang, jolting him into sharp awareness of the world about him, reminding him that the telephone had stopped for a while. He ignored it, snatched a pair of scissors from the dressing table, and cut the taut rope which fastened Felicity's arms to the corners of the bed. Sweat stood out on his forehead.

'I'll kill him,' he muttered savagely. 'I'll smash his face in. The bloody murdering . . .'

The telephone kept on and on.

Dawlish eased Felicity's body down a little, but it did not move. As far as he could see even her muscles did not contract of their own accord. He was almost sobbing. He felt for her pulse while he bent over her and tried to release her legs at the same time, but he could not feel the pulse while doing that, so he stopped.

Was it beating?

If she was dead . . .

He felt as if there were only grief and pain in the whole world.

Was her pulse beating?

Her hand was so limp in his, limp and light. The long narrow fingers with the beautifully shaped scarlet-painted nails were against his massive hand, with the strong fingers and the mat of fair hair on the back.

There was a faint pulse beat; he was sure of it.

'Damn that bloody telephone!' he said viciously.

He let Felicity's hand fall and leaned across at the telephone, only just stopping himself from knocking it flying. An idea lit up in his mind as he lifted the telephone and rasped:

'Who is that?'

'This is Temple, Major. I am sorry to worry you, but—'

'Send a doctor over to my place at once,' Dawlish ordered. 'Tell him it's a case of asphyxia. Warn Westminster Hospital to stand by and to send over an ambulance. All clear?'

After a fraction of a pause Temple said, 'At once, sir.' He rang off before Dawlish.

Dawlish let the cradle clatter back on the telephone and moved back to Felicity. She had not stirred. He pulled at the knot in the sheet at her legs, and it came undone more quickly than he had expected. He tossed it aside, lifted his wife firmly but gently, and put her on the floor just as she had been on the bed. Then he knelt astride her, placed his hands on her ribs, and began to press down with agonising slowness. If he could once get her to start breathing deeply, it might make all the difference. Up and down, up and down, up and down.

After five minutes he could see no change at all in Felicity's pallor, no new evidence of breathing.

'Fel,' he said in a strange, distant voice, 'don't go.'

And a moment later, as sweat dripped off him, 'Fel, for God's sake! Don't go.'

She lay as limp as in death.

Slowly, and with an even greater tension than before, he turned her over. Then he went down on his knees, on his stomach, and lowered his face to hers, pinched her nostrils with one hand, placed his lips on hers, and began to breathe into her mouth, praying that it was into her lungs.

Temple hurried into the entrance of the big building, with Chief Inspector Gordon of the Special Branch by his side. A doorman was waiting for them at the lift. An ambulance bell sounded outside at the same moment.

'I've got the lift ready, sir,' the doorman said.

'Anyone been here?' asked Gordon. He was a thin, round-faced man with red-and-blue-veined white cheeks.

'No, sir.'

'Anyone been out?'

'No, sir.'

'Send the doctor and the ambulance men up at once.'

'Yes, sir.'

Gordon and Temple stepped into the lift, and Gordon pressed the penthouse button. A small notice alongside the button read: DAWLISH.

'Sure it's his wife?' asked Gordon.

'He wouldn't have sounded like that about anyone else.'

'Know him pretty well, don't you?' Gordon sounded curious.

'Well enough to know that if anything's happened to his wife, it'll turn him into the most dangerous man I've ever dealt with.'

'Hmmm.' The lift guide showed that they were on the fifth floor; the penthouses were on the nineteenth. 'Ever pause to think there isn't much difference between a man like Major Dawlish and a professional killer?' Gordon asked.

'Don't talk nonsense,' Temple retorted.

The lift stopped. Across at the foot of the stairs a wallet lay open, with a litter of papers about it. Temple paused. Gordon went on, saying as he reached the stairs: 'I don't want anyone to touch those things. Will you wait here while I take a dekko upstairs?'

'No,' Temple said.

Gordon led the way up. Temple was a couple of yards behind him. They went into the flat, the door of which was wide open. On the floor, lying in an odd position with one leg bent beneath him, was a man whom neither had seen before. In one corner a chair was overturned. Against the pale-green wainscoting was a gun, and near the fallen man's feet was a small hole, quite noticeable in the soft green carpet.

Temple looked at the smashed door of the bedroom.

'Good God!' gasped Gordon, *sotto voce*.

Dawlish lay flat on the floor by the side of his wife, one arm flung across her, one resting against the carpet, a honey-brown colour in here. Felicity Dawlish's body was stretched straight out.

'What a shambles,' Gordon muttered. 'Don't let anyone touch that gun on the floor or that man. I'm going to get a squad over here at the double.'

Dawlish seemed oblivious of both men.

He seemed oblivious, to, when Temple stood in the doorway, when first ambulance men and then a doctor arrived, spoke to him gently, persuaded him to get up. The doctor busied himself; he was a police surgeon and an old friend of Dawlish. 'We'll look after her, Pat,' he said. 'We'll see to her.'

Dawlish stared at him as if afraid to ask the question which was burning in his mind.

'You've got a lot of other things to do, by the look of it,' said the doctor. 'Better get busy.'

He did not say that Felicity would be all right. He did not give Dawlish even a word of reassurance. Dawlish stood on the far side of the bedroom with those magnificent views over London, watching as the ambulance men lifted his beloved, put her on a stretcher, spread a blanket over her, and carried her out.

'I'll send the word as soon as I can,' the police surgeon promised. 'Don't worry.'

He went out, past the squad of Yard men in the little hallway, men who had already chalked off different sections of the hallway and the stairs. Cameras were clicking; an artist was busy with pencil and sketch pad; there was an undertone of voices.

Gordon came in.

'Ready for a statement from you any time you like,' said Gordon.

Dawlish stared at him, seemed to stare through him, and then began to talk in a sharp, clipped voice, stating what happened with a detailed precision which seemed to tell of much rehearsal, although that had not been possible. Gordon was very busy with a pencil and notebook.

Temple stood listening and watching, and the glitter of Dawlish's eyes almost frightened him.

At last Dawlish finished.

'Get your men out as soon as you can, Gordon.' He did not wait for a response but turned to Temple. 'You called me an hour ago. What was it about?'

His voice was cold as stone.

Temple said: 'It may have something to do with this, Major. A man was found shot dead in the Linden Hotel, where—'

Dawlish's self-control threatened to crack at last.

'Van Diesek?'

'Yes,' said Temple. 'And the bullet was fired from a point twenty-three automatic—the size of the automatic lying outside in the other room.'

'So he was after the report,' Dawlish said. 'My God, what a bloody waste! Two girls hammering away at it where he hadn't a chance to lay his hands on it, Van Diesek dead, and my wife—'

He broke off. Temple became vividly aware of Gordon's implication that there was not much difference between Dawlish and a professional killer. Gordon had seen—or imagined—some quality in Dawlish which Temple had never noticed. Now he felt that he did. In Dawlish's expression there was a look of hate, giving an impression of implacable ruthlessness.

He went on: 'All we want are the people who paid him. We don't need telling how to pay them.'

Temple actually shivered.

'Now I want to study that report until I know it off by heart.' Dawlish said.

CHAPTER VI

THE CONFERENCE AGREES

Only a few of the more knowing newspapermen realised that the well-dressed men of various ages who turned into the City Conference Hall next morning were the world's top policemen. They might just as well have been business men or civil servants or delegates to any large conference. Inside the big circular main hall, with its seats in tiers, a desk in front of each, were the inevitable receivers with the tiny earplugs for the interpreters, for not everyone here spoke or understood English perfectly. There was an atmosphere of great tension. At the door Temple received each delegate, who glanced at once at the centre table, where the chairman would sit.

No one was there.

'Is there any news of Mrs. Dawlish?' asked Clare of the Sûreté Nationale. He was a well-dressed, rather sleek man.

'Major Dawlish is at the hospital, *m'sieu.*'

Delgalo of Spain, tall, dark, handsome except for a nasty scar at his lips, said frowningly, 'Is she in danger?'

'I undertand that she had a very bad night, *señor.*'

Van Woelden of the Netherlands, a grey-bearded block of a man, was just behind them.

'Is Dawlish here?'

'He told me that he would be, *mijnheer*.'

'We should send word that we will understand if he cannot come,' said Van Woelden.

'If he decides to come, nothing will keep him away, and if he decides not to, nothing will bring him here,' said Nielson of Sweden.

'Presumably you know the major,' remarked Harrison of New York.

The seats were gradually filled. The murmur of conversation and the rustle of paper increased. Delegate after delegate began to read his copy of the report of Van Diesek's investigation and his request. Heads turned towards heads as the men compared notes and impressions.

With the reports and the agenda was a brief statement about Van Diesek's death and the death of his murderer. The murderer's name was now known as Arthur Donovan, aged thirty-six, a South African of English descent who was known as a car salesman and a commission agent. Word had been sent to Pretoria for more information about him. He had been flown into London on the same plane as Van Diesek. According to the report, he had been killed while Dawlish had fought to get his gun and prevent him from shooting.

Now and again most men glanced at the clocks on the wall, four clocks so that everyone could see in comfort.

The session was due to start at eleven o'clock.

At ten to eleven all but three of the delegates who were due were in their places. Temple watched the bald heads, the grey heads, the black, red, and fair heads. He not only sensed but was highly sensitive to the mood of tension. Not a single man had come in without asking about Dawlish's wife. Temple himself felt as badly as he could; he did not know what could happen to Dawlish if Felicity Dawlish died.

Dawlish had said to him: 'I'll be there. Be sure of that.'

Even now Temple wasn't really sure.

It was one minute to eleven when he had a signal from one of the guards within sight: Dawlish was approaching. As the opening hour approached, a hush fell upon the men and women here, as if by common assent they wanted to wait for Dawlish. Temple thought bleakly that even before this crisis, before the great headlines which had splashed across the morning newspapers, Dawlish had been the best-known man among all of these, the only detective in the world who was known as well as Hoover of the Federal Bureau of Investigation.

Dawlish appeared; his face was like stone.

He did not appear to see Temple, but as he passed he gripped his chief assistant's forearm; the grip was firm but told Temple nothing. Dawlish walked down the shallow steps towards the rostrum. As heads turned he was recognised, and something which Temple had never seen before happened. It had never happened in the history of the Crime Haters.

Every delegate stood up and stood still.

Dawlish passed through the ranks of silent men.

Temple, just behind him, felt tears stinging his eyes. It was a long, long time since he had felt emotion like it. He wondered how Dawlish must be feeling and prayed that the news about Felicity was not worse; for if it was, she was dead.

Dawlish reached the rostrum.

Dawlish had not slept that night.

He had read and reread Van Diesek's report, made notes, checked one point against another, double-checked wherever he could. He did not think there was much in the report he did not now understand, although only Van Diesek, who had lived with the investigation, could have interpreted everything.

He had twice visited and four times telephoned the hospital during the night and had just come from there now. Until he had started this walk he had seen nothing but Felicity's face everywhere, but the spontaneous action of these great policemen wrenched his mind off her. Tears stung his eyes. His lips quivered, although he compressed them tightly. When at last he reached his seat, he was more in control of himself. A young interpreter switched on the microphone. At all costs, Dawlish told himself, he must keep his voice steady.

'Good morning,' he said. 'Please sit down.' He remained standing as the rustle of movement followed. When everyone else was seated, he went on: 'Thank you very much indeed. You will wish to know'—he glanced up, paused, and moistened his lips—'how my wife is. At least I can say that she is no worse. I am not qualified to go into details, but I am told that the pressures on the brain have created a state of coma, and there is no certainty when she will come round from this condition.'

He thought, 'And no certainty that she ever will.'

The mass of people in front of and all about him seemed to merge together, until there was only a conglomeration of heads and faces, eyes and noses, ears and mouths. Savagely he thought, *Get a hold on yourself.* His hands were so tightly clenched that his nails hurt his palms. Then almost to his surprise he found himself saying: 'If any news comes while we are in session I will see that you know at once. Meanwhile I hope you will forgive me if I proceed very quickly with the business of the session. One or two amendments to the agenda first. The minutes of the last session, having been circulated, will not be read, but matters arising may of course be discussed. Item four on the agenda will not now be introduced by Colonel Van Diesek of Pretoria. I have been asked by Pretoria through the High Commissioner in South Africa House to present this myself, and with your permission I will do so from the chair.'

There were a few murmurs of approval, a few raised hands, but no hint of dissent.

'Now,' Dawlish thought, 'I've got to get through this without wondering every minute how she is.'

She was lying absolutely still, inside an oxygen tent. He could picture her. The mask was breathing for her, trying to give her life, as he had tried. Her eyes were closed. Quiet-voiced, soft-footed nurses looked in now and again to have a word with the nurse on duty. Three times in the course of the morning doctors visited her; one a neurologist, one a specialist in respiratory diseases, one a heart specialist.

None was reassured.

Dawlish, on his feet, was saying:

'... There will be plenty of opportunity for everyone to study the report in the evenings or early in the mornings. No one can doubt its quality, the precision, and the care with which it has been drawn up. Van Diesek's death is irreparable, of course. He was the only man who had the whole history of the diamond case in his mind, and we all know that no matter how meticulously a report is made, countless fragmentary items of fact are buried in the mind and cannot be put into a report.' He paused. 'I doubt if anyone will question the gravity of the case. However, when I first heard the figure of a hundred million pounds' worth of diamonds I thought it was over-exaggerated for the sake of emphasis. I am now convinced that it is the correct figure. The report shows how much lower in intrinsic value are the uncut stones. There are a great number of small mines, and for years comparatively small quantities were stolen from each, but there was a considerable cumulative total. Van Diesek began to suspect that the thefts were related some years ago, but his superiors and the United Diamond Distributors were not convinced. He has been accumulating the evidence gradually for a long time. A great number of thefts have been made after the stones have been handed over by the mines to U.D.D. At such time each diamond is marked and ninety per cent of the stolen diamonds have been so marked.'

Dawlish paused. In his mind's eye was a picture of Felicity, and another, of Van Diesek.

'The precautions against theft are uniform and improving year by year. The total value of diamonds mined is so great, and the amount put into storage so vast, that in the early years the percentage loss was not worrying. Some big thefts quite recently have added to the total, so much that if Van Diesek was right, and they have been accumulated against a sudden release on world markets, the effect would be extremely serious. Van Diesek finally convinced his superiors of this.

'Then there is no way yet of knowing whether any such distribution is planned or whether these stones are already being placed upon the market in large quantities. All we know, and that is on circumstantial evidence which I don't question, is that theft on such a vast and long-term scale would only have been perpetrated by criminals who have every confidence in their ability to sell and distribute. Just as there exists a world organisation handling opium and another dealing in counterfeit currency, so there may be one about to handle diamonds. Does anyone disagree?'

No one spoke.

Dawlish went on: 'Thank you. I think the discussion should begin.'

After a pause a tall, lean-faced man with curly hair stood up at the back of the room. He was Carter, from Sydney, perhaps Australia's best-known Criminal Investigation Bureau superintendent.

'I don't think there's much to discuss, Mr. Chairman. We've got to get into this case quick. I'm worried about one thing.'

'What's that?'

'Is there anyone from South Africa to replace Van Diesek?'

Dawlish said, 'No.'

'Surely we need to hear from Pretoria.' That was Castleton, the Southern Rhodesian delegate.

'If they send Van Diesek's second-in-command for this session, it will waste time,' Dawlish said. 'This case needs a working party from the Conference to go to South Africa as soon as possible. A start today wouldn't be too soon.'

Someone with a guttural voice said, 'Ach, yes.'

'We need the Conference to agree to give the case priority and to commit all national police headquarters to assist and then men on the spot to work with the South Africans,' Dawlish went on. 'Is there any other suggestion?'

'I guess it's the only way,' Harrison conceded. 'But there's plenty more to worry about.'

'In what way?'

'Where are they most likely to unload the loot?' asked Harrison. 'Amsterdam? London? New York? Or maybe one of the free ports, like Aden or Hong Kong? We need to get every national headquarters busy checking outlets. So we need a working party on the spot and one in the Conference, to help the secretariat. Any word of an extra pile of diamonds coming on the market, and we need to be ready to act.'

Sobolov of Russia said in his unexpectedly good English, 'I am in full agreement with that.'

'Two working parties,' Dawlish said. 'Proposed by New York, seconded by Moscow.' The faintest of smiles played at the corner of his lips. 'Any amendment to that?'

No one spoke.

'Then we'll put it to the vote,' Dawlish said. 'A show of hands will do. Those in favour?'

A forest of hands shot up. There was no need to count, and Dawlish's 'Any against?' was simply a formality. As Temple entered the item into his book, Dawlish thought fleetingly of how gratified Van Diesek would have been. Would there have been such unanimity without the Afrikaner's death? Or without the attack on Felicity?

One of the two telephones near him glowed, its light replacing the ringing sound. Dawlish's thoughts flew to the hospital. His jaws clamped together. He lifted the receiver while there was the inevitable rustle of relaxation after a decision had been made.

'This is Major Dawlish.'

'Hallo, Pat. This is Coombs,' the elderly police surgeon who had been the first to see Felicity. 'I'm not going to make the situation any worse for you.'

Dawlish almost barked, 'How is she?'

'She's round from the deep coma,' Coombs said. 'She's still very weak and certainly not out of danger, but there's no longer any likelihood of a sudden collapse. She reacted well enough to convince us that she is likely to come through. It will be a long, slow business. I won't go into technicalities, but the pressures have set up a traumatic condition, which—'

'How long?' Dawlish asked brusquely,

'I would only be guessing.'

'Days? Weeks? Months?'

'Certainly weeks,' Coombs said.

After a short pause Dawlish spoke a little less tensely.

'Thanks, Doc. Just one thing. Will I be able to help if I'm close by?'

'I doubt if she'll even know whether you're around for the next two or three weeks,' answered Coombs.

'Thanks.' Dawlish almost choked. 'Doc, I—'

''Bye, Pat,' Coombe said and rang off.

Dawlish put the receiver down slowly. He was not aware of the hush at first; he could only think of the news. Felicity would be all right. Then he realised everyone was looking at him and no one was moving or speaking. He closed his eyes for a moment, then stood up slowly. His voice was clear and quiet.

'The immediate danger to my wife is over.' He paused only for a moment and went on to make sure there could be no outburst of emotion from reaction. 'We have two working parties to select. I think we should follow custom and call first for volunteers. And I hope I will be forgiven for breaking with custom and volunteering from the chair to go with the party to South Africa.'

Temple thought: 'It was inevitable. He's got to see this thing through himself.'

Dawlish thought, 'I wonder how soon I can get away.'

Then Harrison of New York and Van Woelden of Amsterdam volunteered almost in the same breath.

On that particular day Della Forrest felt better than she had for over a week. Her throat, badly bruised from the cruel pressure of the man who had nearly killed her and nearly killed Nigel, felt almost free from pain. She could turn her head fairly freely, too. The night before she had slept without a nightmare, without waking up with an awful feeling of suffocation, as if she could still feel the man's fingers round her neck.

She no longer slept in the same room as Nigel.

Nigel was in a room at Ma Parkin's, and Ma was looking after him with the full approval of the doctor who had come out from Buckingham. Ma was doing a first-class job, the doctor said. Nigel was on the mend too. He still had a temperature and was in a semi-coma; it would be a month or more before he was likely to get about, but he was out of danger.

He had not yet recognised her or anyone. He had not yet spoken a word. Even the snowy-haired young lieutenant of police who had come out from Kimberley to question Della about the attack had not been able to get a word out of Nigel.

It was as if he had been struck dumb.

The lieutenant and his one assistant, both Afrikaners, had stayed for two days, asked innumerable probing questions, taken photographs, taken fingerprints and turned the spotless little home upside down. They had questioned everyone in the town, too—including Jeff Mason.

A difficult thing for Della to accept was that she and Nigel now owed their lives to Jeff. He had been sleeping in a tent in the grounds, unknown to anyone, in case she needed help in the night.

Her scream had brought him running.

But the hardest thing for Della to accept was her own attitude towards Nigel. Every time she saw him she hoped she would feel differently, but each time she felt as if she were looking into the face of a stranger.

She hated herself for it, but there was nothing she could do except hope her attitude would soon change.

CHAPTER VII

THE FINGERPRINTS

'Major Dawlish, please!'

'Hold it!'

'Just one more.'

'How is your wife, Major?'

'What's it all about, Dawlish?'

The questions at the Jan Smuts Airport came thick and fast. The cameras clicked and flashed. A crowd of at least thirty newspapermen crowded into the big room at the airport, where Dawlish towered above everyone else except a very blond young lieutenant from the South Africa Police Headquarters at Pretoria, there to welcome the working party. It was a hot, clear, beautiful day.

'Did Van Diesek come to see you, Major?'

'What's in this for us?'

'What's it all about, Major Dawlish?'

Dawlish said mildly. 'If you'd stop shouting for a minute, I might be able to get a word in.'

'What's that?'

'Quiet, there!'

'*Quiet!*'

Dawlish smiled more freely.

'Thanks,' he said. 'Question one—what's it all about? That's no secret—diamonds. Your police aren't happy about security measures in the Republic and think a lot of the little beauties are getting out when they should be kept in. The question is: where do they go? That's what we hope to help find out.'

When he stopped there was another barrage of questions. Dawlish simply shook his head, until a woman reporter asked clearly: 'Are you here on a matter of personal revenge, Major?'

'No,' said Dawlish. 'I am here as a policeman.'

'The attack on your wife has nothing to do with your arrival here?'

'The murder of one of your leading police officers has much more to do with it.'

'Wouldn't you rather have stayed by your wife's side, Major Dawlish?'

Dawlish said: 'Yes. So would any policeman, soldier, sailor, or airman in the same dilemma.' He smiled at the blond young police officer. 'Do you think we could go?'

Questions were fired at him as the little group made its way to the car waiting outside the low-built airport buildings. More reporters and photographers and a considerable crowd were there, but more policemen in khaki uniform were waiting, and no more time was lost. Three police cars moved off at the same speed, Dawlish and the other two men who had flown from London in the middle one.

Wade Harrison, who was comparatively new in the Crime Haters organisation, looked at Van Woelden, one of the founder members.

'Can you beat that? About a thousand questions and not one of them for you or me. Didn't anyone tell them this was a working party?'

'When you work with Dawlish you get used to that,' Van Woelden retorted.

'Is that right?' Harrison cocked a speculative eye at Dawlish. Harrison was a tall, dark man, good-looking in a sharp-featured way. At moments he reminded Dawlish of the man who had attacked Felicity and killed Van Diesek. It was only a fleeting resemblance, but Dawlish wished it did not exist. At the moment he wondered what the American was thinking. Had the attitude of the reporters annoyed, even angered him? Policemen were human, a fact which many people forgot. They suffered from the normal jealousy, envy, and resentment like everyone else. He wished he knew Harrison better.

'It comes in useful,' Dawlish remarked.

'How's that?'

'If I get all the spotlight, you can stay right out of the public eye. Everywhere I go I'll be recognised. You won't necessarily.'

'I suppose.' Harrison did not sound convinced.

Dawlish caught the Dutchman's eye and thought the same doubts were passing through his mind. Then Harrison's attention was caught by two natives at the side of the road, women with babies on their backs huddled in blankets. He leaned forward as if he couldn't believe his eyes. Dawlish and Van Woelden made no comment, and before Harrison could speak two cars came towards them at an alarming speed. The police driver swung the wheel to avoid a collision.

'Pat,' Harrison said suddenly, as if all thought of jealousy was ridiculous, 'do you think you fooled those newspapermen?'

'Part of the time.'

'They know it's big. I wouldn't like to say what they will do if they even guess how big.' After a pause Harrison added, 'Do you know where we're going to start?'

'Visit the places where the diamonds were stolen,' Dawlish said.

Harrison pulled at his upper lip.

'I can't wait to get started. One hundred million pounds' worth—three hundred million dollars' worth. You want to know something?'

'Yes,' Dawlish said.

'These guys think bigger than Americans! There aren't many men who could be trusted with that kind of money,' went on Harrison. 'Not many security forces are so well paid that one or two members wouldn't be glad to sell a little information. In the report Van Diesek said he had absolute confidence in the security arrangements and personnel. I'm not so sure he was right. Are you receptive to ideas?'

'Try me,' Dawlish said cautiously, hopefully.

'Why don't you let me loose among the security people at the various mines? I'm good at making myself unpopular. You keep out of that so we can preserve the image of the infallible Patrick Dawlish, everybody's blue-eyed boy?'

There was a core of good sound sense in the suggestion. Was there also a knife edge of malice?

'I think that is the way to work,' Van Woelden agreed, as if to give Dawlish no time to wonder. 'I will stay here and co-ordinate. Harrison will go to the mines. You, Dawlish, will work on the man Donovan. Is that all right?'

'It's fine with me,' Harrison said.

'It should work,' said Dawlish.

Colonel Voort, Chief of Police at Pretoria, was an elderly, quiet-voiced, watchful individual, the type whom the Yard would dub 'Uncle'. In ten minutes he convinced Dawlish that he had a complete grasp of the situation. He sat at one side of the large pedestal desk, with the blond lieutenant and a dumpy-looking shorthand writer by his side. Dawlish and Van Woelden and

Harrison sat on the other side of the desk, Van Woelden in the middle.

Dawlish had feared a long preamble and time-taking formalities. Once in here he lost those fears but sensed something else: a kind of tension, perhaps over-eagerness, in the lieutenant. It showed in his quick glances at every man who spoke, in the tension of his hands as his fists clenched.

'The two matters which worry us most concern the theft itself and the disposition of the diamonds,' Colonel Voort said. 'I do not need to labour any point in Van Diesek's report, I am sure.'

'It couldn't be more concise,' Dawlish agreed.

'If it's all right with you, I'll go back over the later thefts.' Harrison did not wait for either of the others to say his piece for him. 'If anyone can take away three million dollars' worth of diamonds, that's bad security.'

'The mine authorities won't agree with you,' Voort said dryly. 'But they will welcome anyone who can help them to strengthen it. Will you start at the mines, gentlemen?'

The lieutenant's lips moved, as if he wanted to protest. Voort almost certainly saw him but took no notice.

'I'd rather like to concentrate on the man who killed Van Diesek,' Dawlish said.

The lieutenant's eyes seemed to snap approval.

Voort gave a benevolent little smile and turned to the younger man.

'Lieutenant Bukas will undoubtedly agree with you—won't you, Lieutenant?'

'With the Colonel's approval,' said the lieutenant.

Dawlish wondered how old he was; he looked in his early twenties but must be thirty or so. He had very fair, almost snowy hair, pale-blue eyes, pale lashes, and a complexion any woman would be proud of, yet there was nothing remotely feminine about him.

'You have it,' Voort said dryly.

'Thank you, sir.' Lieutenant Bukas drew himself to attention and stared at Dawlish, as if oblivious of Harrison's half-amused, half-cynical appraisal and Van Woelden's critical expression. 'It was my duty recently to investigate an attempted murder in a small dorp in the southern Kalahari. In the course of the routine investigation I found certain fingerprints.' He leaned forward, opened a manila folder on his desk, and revealed two sets of fingerprint photographs. He turned these so all three members of the Conference could see not only the prints but some red lines and numerals.

'You see, gentlemen?' Bukas pointed with his forefinger; he had a long, well-shaped hand. 'There are eleven points of similarity, proving conclusively that these are the fingerprints of the same man. *These*'—he stubbed his finger at the darker print—'were found at the house where an attempt was made to strangle a young woman and to suffocate her husband, who was at one time a diamond cutter.'

Dawlish's heart seemed to contract at the word *strangle*. Bukas stabbed at a lighter print.

'And that is the print of the man Donovan, whom you killed after his attack on your wife.'

Now Dawlish's heart began to thump. He felt for the first time that there seemed a prospect of real progress; this fair-haired youngster was giving him the starting point he needed so desperately. He had never felt more intent, more grimly determined, to solve a case. The twin motives, of revenge for Felicity and of the need to find the criminals who had employed Donovan, were inextricably mixed up in his mind.

He was aware of silence. He broke through the tension which

had gripped him and realised that the others were all staring at him—even Voort. He made himself speak equably.

'Where are the man and woman?'

'They are in an isolated town in the Kalahari.'

'How soon can we get to this place?'

'We can fly to Buckingham, where there is an airstrip. From there it is three hours by road to Kangarmie,' Bukas said. There was a puzzled expression in his eyes when he spoke, as he looked at Dawlish. The others were still staring at him too.

'When can we catch the plane?' Dawlish asked.

'One is available at any time at the airport,' Voort said. 'We expected you would wish to go there today.' He stood up. 'You have my assurance of the utmost co-operation while you are here. If you can help us to find any quantity of the diamonds, and those who stole them, we will be for ever in your debt.'

He sounded as if he meant it from his heart.

'Now, I have luncheon arranged for you in a private room where you can have any confidential discussion you wish.'

'Pat,' said Wade Harrison quietly, 'how often do you kill vital witnesses?'

'Now, Harrison . . .' Van Woelden began.

'Stop protecting the guy. He's a big boy now. He can speak for himself,' Harrison said laconically. 'I mean witnesses such as Donovan.'

'I must ask you—' Van Woelden began.

'I'm just asking if Major Dawlish knows his own strength,' Harrison went on. 'It's a fair question. You've known him a long time. I haven't been indoctrinated yet.'

Dawlish pushed his coffee cup away.

'If Donovan had lived, he might have talked,' he said. 'So I didn't help the cause along by hitting him so hard.'

'You certainly did not.'

'And if I get near enough to someone else, you want to know if there's a danger that I might hit them too hard too?'

'That's my question,' Harrison agreed. 'I don't think I would have asked if you hadn't reacted the way you did when you heard that Donovan's prints had been found in this desert what-did-he-call-it?'

'A dorp,' Dawlish frowned. 'Was I as bad as that?'

'You were worse.'

Dawlish turned to Van Woelden.

'Worse than usual?'

'I don't like to say so,' Van Woelden answered, 'but you looked as if you couldn't wait to kill.'

Harrison let out an explosive little laugh.

'I always did appreciate straight talk.'

'Yes,' Dawlish said. 'So did I. I still do. I'll watch myself.' He could have added that there was so much in extenuation: the awful pressures of the moment, the agonising decision he had been forced to make in a fraction of a second. There was no point in such excuses. He wanted to find these criminals as he had never wanted to find criminals in the past. There was indeed a danger that if he caught up with them he would be tempted to deal out summary justice.

Only it wouldn't be justice. He had to guard against himself as well as the enemy.

CHAPTER VIII

THE DORP

It was a two-seater plane, with young Bukas at the controls. He handled them perfectly, but that wasn't difficult, for the weather was perfect for flying. For half an hour they had flown over scrub-filled desert land, with only a few outcrops of rock to break the monotony. Here and there they saw a mine or a farm, with its water windmill the tell-tale indication every time.

Bukas said very little.

Dawlish had thought a great deal.

A small town showed up in the distance against the afternoon sun, and it seemed only a minute or so before Bukas turned his head and mouthed, 'Seat belt.'

Dawlish strapped his on. The little aircraft began to lose height. An antiquated fire truck stood near a wooden building, with two men by it. They proved to be the only two men at the airfield, one of them a mechanic and maintenance worker, one of them a policeman. Just outside the shed was a black Mercedes, and Bukas in the searing heat of the sun led the way to this.

'You'll come and have tea before you go to Kangarmie,' the local man said.

Bukas' expression seemed to plead, 'Don't let us waste any time.'

'If we leave now, we will be there before dark,' he said.

'I'll be glad to wait for tea until we get there,' Dawlish said.

The local man shrugged and opened the door. The car was stifling hot inside, the leather seat burning. The sun had caught a part of the steering wheel and Bukas snatched his hand away, took out a handkerchief, and folded it.

He started off as if only speed mattered.

Dawlish wondered what was driving him. Ambition? Temperament? He was an Afrikaner but lacked the deliberation which characterised most of those whom Dawlish knew. He was a handsome young chap in his blond way but driven as by devils.

Suddenly he said, 'Major Dawlish.'

'Yes, Lieutenant.'

'Colonel Van Diesek was a good friend of mine.'

'Ah,' murmured Dawlish.

'He might have been my father, he took so much trouble to help me.'

'He was a good man.'

'He was a great detective,' Bukas declared in a tone of restrained passion. 'There is nothing I desire more than to avenge him.'

Dawlish said, 'I think I can understand that.'

He wondered what Harrison would say if he could overhear this conversation.

'Major Dawlish,' Bukas went on, 'I believe the colonel was killed because he alone had such a knowledge of the crimes caused by diamond thieves in this country. His mind was like an electronic machine; whenever facts were discussed about diamonds, all the related factors came together in his mind. There was no one else like him. He had a very clever assistant who was killed in an accident last year. He was driving his own car and was known to be a fast driver, but—'

Dawlish murmured, 'Was he murdered too?'

'I know that Colonel Van Diesek thought it possible,' Bukas said. 'Anyone with a deep, exhaustive knowledge of diamond smuggling and theft is now dead.'

For the first time Dawlish wondered whether Van Diesek's report was the true motive for the murder in London. But if it wasn't—why had Felicity been attacked?

Della Forrest stood on the stoep and watched the black car coming away from the Parkins' store. She could not yet be sure that it was heading here, but it was probable. She could not see how many men were in the car, but one thing was certain: it was a car from out of town. There was nothing so new and shiny-looking in Kangarmie.

It was seven o'clock, early for a stranger unless they had stayed at Ma Parkin's overnight. The last time Della had seen a black car like this had been when the lieutenant of police had come from Kimberley. She wondered if this was him again.

She went inside and put on a kettle. Her actions were mechanical, as they had been for so long, but her whole mood had changed. For over two years she had done nothing but wait for Nigel and think of him. Now she tried not to think of anything.

It was awful, shameful. At least no one else knew.

She heard the crunch of the wheels, tidied her hair deftly in the mirror, and went to the door. As she opened it, the fair-haired lieutenant was getting out of the car, and another man was already standing by the side of it. He was huge—one of the biggest and tallest men she had ever seen. He was staring at the door and so at her, and she thought she had never seen a man so impressive or so magnificently handsome. He was fair-haired, too, but his hair was the colour of corn, crisp and wavy. He wore a long-sleeved white shirt and city trousers—obviously he hadn't come prepared for the desert.

She could hardly take her eyes off him.

'She's a pretty kid,' thought Dawlish.

As he drew nearer, he smiled in the way which so many people found attractive, particularly young women. She had dark, rather fluffy hair, a heart-shaped face, nice lips, nice honey-brown eyes. She wore a simple dress of pale-yellow colour which hung straight from the shoulders, falling gently over her bosom; she had quite a figure.

Young Bukas came hurrying.

'Mrs. Forrest, I am sorry to have to worry you again. This is Major Dawlish, from England. He also needs to ask you a few questions.'

'From England?' Della's eyes lit up. Anyone from England might be a messenger from home.

'Come in.' She stood aside and they passed quickly.

Dawlish took one glance about the room and knew that pretty little Mrs. Forrest was as proud of her house as Felicity. Felicity. She had something of Felicity's manner and looks, too; she wasn't a beauty in the accepted sense, but wholesome and attractive. He had heard the story of her long vigil, her faith, and her patience. It was quite a story.

They had something in common too. Her husband lay in a semi-coma, just as Felicity in England; he had seen him twice, last night and this morning. He was suffering from an acute form of heat exhaustion and might have to be moved to the hospital in Kimberley, the nearest town of any size.

Bukas was already explaining.

'. . . and if you will describe exactly what happened to Major Dawlish . . .'

Dawlish saw the repugnance in the girl's eyes. He could imagine what a nightmare it had been and how much she hated retelling and so reliving all that had happened.

'I don't think I can improve on your report about that,' he said to Bukas. 'I'm interested in where your husband went, Mrs. Forrest, and what he said to you when he came back.'

'But he said nothing.'

'Not a word?' asked Dawlish. 'Not a single word?'

'If he had, I would have told the lieutenant before.' Della Forrest looked almost angrily at Bukas, as if blaming him for not having convinced Dawlish. 'My husband hasn't spoken since he came back—not to me, not to anyone.'

Dawlish was sitting down in a large cane chair. Bukas stood by the window where the Venetian blinds were down. The room was already warm, although the sun was not yet high. The girl—she wasn't much more than a girl—stood facing them. There was something about her manner which puzzled Dawlish—a tension which suggested that her husband's home-coming had not solved all her emotional problems.

Somewhere nearby there was a hissing sound. In the quiet the girl heard it and said, 'I will make some tea.' She hurried into the kitchen, leaving the door open. Dawlish could see her moving about.

'Did she resent being questioned before?' Dawlish asked Bukas.

'Resent? No.'

'Was she as keyed up as this?'

'Keyed up?'

'Edgy.'

'No,' said Bukas. 'She was more dazed, I think.'

'How often does she go and see her husband?'

'At least once each day.'

'Once a day, and he's only half a mile or so away.' Dawlish mused. 'I wonder if—'

He broke off as the girl came back carrying a tea tray, biscuits, sugar, milk, and lemon. She put this down on the table near him, looking more self-possessed.

'Have you found the man who attacked us?' she asked.

Dawlish countered, 'Will you look at this?' He handed her a photograph taken out of his pocket almost with a sleight of hand. It was Donovan, photographed in death but looking as if he were asleep.

The girl took it.

'I did not see him, except just a glimpse when I woke up. And he was upside down to me, remember—he was standing behind me.'

'Ah,' said Dawlish. He stood up very quickly, startling her, took the photograph, and twisted it round so that she looked at it as if Donovan was upside down.

Della caught her breath.

'Well?' demanded Dawlish.

'It might be him.'

'Have you ever seen him before that night?'

'Never.'

'Has he ever been here?'

'If he had. I would have known.'

'Unless he came to see your husband when you weren't here.'

She said almost bitterly: 'Nigel was never here on his own. He had no idea what it was like to sit and wait and—' She broke off.

Dawlish said sharply: 'We must have the truth, Mrs. Forrest. It's essential.'

'I *am* telling you the truth.'

'Have you ever seen this man before?'

'No!' she cried, backing away from Dawlish, as if suddenly he was frightening her. Bukas looked puzzled, as if he could not understand Dawlish's aggressive tactics. Dawlish now felt sure that the girl was living on her nerves, that she would never be able to keep anything back if he exerted enough pressure. It was essential—it was vital—to make quite sure that she was telling the truth. The right tactics now might save a lot of time and trouble later.

'Have you ever heard the name Donovan?' he asked.

She didn't answer but stood breathing hard.

'*Donovan*. You heard me,' repeated Dawlish roughly.

'I—I've heard the name, yes.'

'Do you know anyone called Donovan?'

'No.'

'Are you sure?'

'Of course I'm sure!' she cried. 'Why should I lie to you?'

'That's what I mean to find out,' Dawlish said.

She turned to Bukas as if in appeal, but he sat still and silent.

'Do you know a man named Donovan?' Dawlish demanded again.

More quietly Della replied, 'No, I don't.'

'But the name is familiar.'

'Yes,' she said. 'Yes.' She turned to look out of the window, and when she spoke again it was as if the words were drawn out of her, causing great pain. 'My husband knew a man named Donovan. He once went prospecting with him. He was going with him again. He left here to meet Donovan and was away for two years and two months and three days.'

There was deep bitterness in her voice which startled Dawlish. But Bukas almost certainly missed it—he was so elated at the news that Nigel Forrest knew the man who had murdered Colonel Van Diesek.

* * *

'He was away for two years and two months and three days.'

The bitterness in Della Forrest's voice made Dawlish study her more closely. The edginess might spring from a variety of causes, from guilt of some kind to deep resentment. She spoke almost as if she blamed her husband for his long absence, yet the touching story of her patient, unshakable faith in his return seemed to tell a different story.

Bukas, obviously eager to make some comment, did not say a word; he was the perfectly disciplined junior officer. Dawlish took advantage of his patience.

'This could be of great importance, Mrs. Forrest. Are you sure that your husband went to meet Donovan?'

'Yes, I am.'

'Did he meet him?'

'I don't know.'

'Didn't he say so when he wrote to you?'

'He didn't write to me.'

Dawlish was startled.

'Not once in over two years? Even in the early days?'

'Not once,' Della averred. 'Not in all that time.'

Bukas made a little noise, as if he were as shaken as Dawlish. Dawlish marvelled that her faith had stood the long silence and was more than ever puzzled by her present manner and her present mood.

'Do you know what he was going to do?'

Della didn't answer.

'Mrs. Forrest, it is important that you should tell us—' Dawlish began.

'Why is it so important?' she interrupted. 'Who are you? What do you want? A man came here, nearly killed me, nearly killed Nigel. Isn't that enough? Can't I ever have a moment's peace without questions, questions questions?' She began to move about the room, in short, jerky steps. Bukas watched every movement she made, but Dawlish leaned back and stared at the ceiling. When she went on her voice was higher, as if her nerves were at breaking point. 'Why don't you ask Nigel?'

She stood in front of Dawlish, but he did not look at her, he still stared at the ceiling, as if determined to ignore what she said.

'Answer me!' she cried 'Why don't you ask Nigel? Why don't you make him talk? Why come to me?'

Bukas could keep quiet no longer.

'He is not able to talk yet. He might not talk for several days, perhaps for weeks. It might be too late then.'

'Too late for what?' Della screamed.

Dawlish sat upright and turned his gaze towards her.

'A very large quantity of diamonds have been stolen, Mrs. Forrest. We know that the man Donovan was involved in the theft. We want to find everyone who helped him, and we want to find out where he has been recently. What can you tell us?'

She stood standing in front of him, looking appalled.

'Diamonds,' she breathed.

'A lot of diamonds.'

She caught her breath. Bukas was on his feet, hands outstretched as if in eager appeal.

'Diamonds,' Della repeated, and Dawlish could only just hear the word. 'He promised me diamonds, when he came back he had nothing, nothing, nothing. He promised me diamonds. He said I could have all the diamonds in the world.'

CHAPTER IX

DELLA

Bukas cried, 'So he knew what was going to happen!'

'Easy,' said Dawlish.

'But he must have known.'

'Be quiet!'

'No,' said Della choking. 'No, he wouldn't have planned to steal them. He wouldn't have stolen anything.' Tears filled her eyes and gave them a greater depth of colour. Her lips were working as if she could hardly keep them steady. 'He isn't a thief. Not Nigel.' She faltered, and as Dawlish moved to get up she seemed to drop towards him, arms groping as if in need of physical support. There was Dawlish sitting upright with the girl's arms around his neck, her head against his shoulder. She began to cry in deep, racking sobs.

Bukas muttered something under his breath.

Dawlish slid his left arm round the girl's waist and mouthed to Bukas, 'Can you make some fresh tea?'

After a moment's pause Bukas said: 'Tea? Yes, of course.'

He picked up the tea tray and went out.

Dawlish did not move. The girl's body pressed tightly against him, and he could feel the fullness of her breast. The sobs seemed to come from deep within her. The pressure of her arms about his neck increased. It did not seem as if she could stop crying.

Dawlish began to smooth the back of her head with his right hand. Slowly, very slowly, the paroxysm eased. He did not try to make her move but felt the slow relaxing of her tension. He stroked her hair, gently, soothingly.

Soon, no longer crying, she drew away. Tears smeared her cheeks and reddened her eyes, which were puffy, like her lips. She hid her face in both hands as if suddenly aware of what a sight she might look. Dawlish stood up and moved away.

'It'll be all right,' he said gently. 'Just hold on, Della. Just hold on.'

He went into the kitchen. Bukas had put on the kettle, which was nearly boiling. He was standing in the doorway and looked very young and strikingly handsome in his scrubbed pink-and-white way.

'The husband is involved.'

'It looks like it.'

'There can't be any doubt!'

Dawlish smiled wryly as he said, 'Colonel Van Diesek wouldn't have said that on the evidence we've got now.'

'But Forrest promised her diamonds!'

'Doesn't every man in love promise his beloved diamonds?'

Bukas hesitated, as if considering this for the first time, and then said in a more subdued voice: 'Surely not. Unless you mean figuratively.'

'I do.'

'But Forrest said *diamonds*.'

'Yes.' After a pause Dawlish went on, almost to himself, 'How long will it be before Forrest can talk?'

'The doctor says it might be any time after the next day or two. When he comes round, full recovery should be quick.'

'I hope so,' Dawlish said. 'I wonder what else his wife knows.'

'Do you think she knows anything more?'

'She knew about diamonds, and about Donovan, even if she didn't realise their significance,' Dawlish said. 'Deep down in her memory she probably knows a lot more?'

'So that is why you questioned her so roughly. To make her begin to think.'

'That's it,' Dawlish said. 'With luck she's thinking already. I'll be more gentle next time.'

Bukas said bleakly, 'The important thing is to get results.'

'Yes.' Dawlish changed the subject. 'Will you go down to the village and try to find out in what direction Nigel Forrest went and where he was heading? Someone must know something. He may have talked to the garage people or to the Parkins when he bought his stores. He was provisioned for three months, wasn't he?'

'Yes.' Bukas stood up, ever ready to be on the move. 'I will go at once and return here as soon as I have finished.'

'There's no great hurry,' Dawlish said.

He eased his collar away from his neck; this was a dry day but with a sticky heat. It was very hot in here, and the steaming kettle probably accounted for the humidity. He made fresh tea and took it into the living room. As he put it on the table, the bedroom door opened.

Della looked a different woman.

She had brushed and combed her hair until it was a sleek and shiny cluster about her head. She had got rid of all the signs of crying, except a faint redness and puffiness at her eyes. She looked fresh and quite delightful, and again she reminded Dawlish of Felicity.

She smiled, as if without too much effort.

'Come and sit down and have a cup of tea,' Dawlish said.

'Oh, that will be stewed.'

'It's fresh,' he assured her.

She looked startled, then gave a rather brittle laugh.

'What's funny?' inquired Dawlish.

'The thought of you making tea. Are you sure you wouldn't prefer cold beer?'

'I certainly would prefer beer.'

She laughed again, on the same note. 'I thought you would. And I've got some iced tea in the fridge.' She went to the kitchen, picking up the tray as she went. 'this won't be wasted. I'll let it get cool and then ice it.'

Dawlish followed, watched her busy, practical movements and the methodical way she pierced a can of beer. She handed it to him with a porcelain tankard. When they were back in the living room she said matter-of-factly: 'I always kept cold beer ready for Nigel. Ma Parkin was very good. She changed it every two weeks.'

'Nice of her,' Dawlish said. 'It must have been very lonely.'

'It was.'

'Had you given him up?'

'Not really,' Della said after a pause. 'I just couldn't believe he would walk out of my life like that.'

'You were right,' remarked Dawlish. He was biding his time for the moment when he could get her to talk again; it would be much better if she began of her own accord.

She was looking at him very intently, and he knew that her calmness was simply on the surface—she was still a seething emotional tangle inside. But she had regained her self-control, which was all-important.

'Major Dawlish, if I tell you something personal, will you promise not to tell anyone else?'

'Provided it doesn't affect the inquiry—yes, of course I promise.'

'Oh, it doesn't. I feel I can tell you because—well, you're English and you're a stranger—really a stranger. I suppose when this is all over you'll go away and I'll never see you again.'

'That's quite likely.'

'It's a very simple thing,' Della went on, 'and yet it's awful. I hate myself for it, and yet there's nothing I can do about it. I waited so long for Nigel that my whole life depended on that day. Then—then he came back and—and I don't feel anything.' She sounded forlorn and woebegone, rather than distressed. 'I don't feel anything at all.'

'Don't you, Della?' asked Dawlish very gently.

'I don't feel anything at all, I tell you. It's as if Nigel is a stranger. I don't love him. I don't really care about him. I can't understand it, unless—unless it was because he looked so awful when I first saw him. You've seen him, haven't you?'

Dawlish had seen a skeleton of a man, lying motionless.

'Yes,' he said.

'He—he was much worse when he first came back.'

'I can well believe it.'

'I thought you would be able to,' she said chokily. 'He looked like a death's-head.'

Dawlish didn't speak.

'A death's-head,' she repeated in a quivery voice. 'His clothes were like rags. He couldn't have weighed more than sixty or seventy pounds. When he went away he weighed a hundred and fifty. It was awful, the day he came back—awful. But in a way it's worse now, because I can't make myself care for him. I just can't.'

Her voice broke, as if her control was going to crack again.

'I think you'll be all right,' Dawlish said. 'It's a form of shock.'

'It was an awful shock!'

'And a collapse from tension of waiting,' added Dawlish matter-of-factly.

'But what shall I do?'

'What you're so good at doing,' Dawlish said. 'Just wait for events. Don't be impatient now. You need your patience more than ever.'

Tears were making her eyes glisten.

'I suppose I do, but it's not so easy as it was. Then I was waiting for something I understood, something I believed would happen. Now I don't know what to believe or what to expect. Major Dawlish—'

'Yes?'

'Do you think Nigel's a thief?'

'I know Donovan was,' said Dawlish thoughtfully. Della had come round to the subject without prompting, and that was just what he had wanted. 'You know far more about Nigel too. The evidence so far here says that he wasn't a thief.'

She looked startled.

'Here? In this house?'

'There isn't much evidence of a successful career of crime, is there?'

She stared, not at first comprehending, then broke into a more natural laugh.

'Oh, he hadn't any money!'

'None?'

'Very little, anyhow,' Della said. 'He used to work for one or other of the copper and asbestos miners near here, or he'd do some rock testing for gold and uranium—the big companies pay a good fee. I've a few hundred pounds a year of my own too.'

'No, he didn't make money from crime.'

'That doesn't mean that he wouldn't have tried,' Della said

logically. 'He always dreamed of finding diamonds, I know that. Diamonds fascinated him more than gold or anything else.'

'Did he talk much about them?'

'Sometimes,' she said. 'He was apprenticed to a diamond cutter once but gave it up. He had always promised me diamonds. He didn't realise that I just wanted him, I didn't care what he had. He always had to go looking for the moon and I didn't even mind that.'

'How often did he go away?'

'Most months,' she said. 'We lived here for five years. At first I hated it, but I grew to love the desert. I still do. He used to work for three weeks and go away for one. At first he was sure he'd strike it lucky, but towards the end he didn't say much. He just used to go off. I think he was afraid of admitting that he was beaten. Then he stayed home for two months, and I thought he was going to give up. I think he would have but for the letter.'

'Letter?'

'From Donovan.'

Dawlish fought back a rising excitement.

'About the prospecting?'

'Yes. Donovan said he was sure he'd found blue ground and offered Nigel a half share if he would help him work it.'

'Did he say where?'

'No.'

'Do you mean that Nigel didn't tell you or Donovan didn't tell him?' Excitement crept into his voice.

'Donovan just said they were to meet at the place they'd worked together before. Nigel said it was about a hundred miles south-west and he could find the spot blindfold.'

'Did he describe it?'

Della frowned as if trying to recollect.

'Does it matter?' she asked slowly.

'It could matter a great deal.'

Della frowned, leaning forward, elbow on her knees, one hand at her chin. Most of her tension had gone. Talking had helped; confiding in Dawlish had helped even more. Her honey-brown eyes were clear and lovely.

'Yes, he certainly described it, Major Dawlish. He plotted the course on a map. I remember he said not only that it was about a hundred miles south-west but that the trail marks were some big rocks, a baobab tree, some old mines—a small vein of gold was found there once—and a range of black hills.' After a pause she added, 'Will that help?'

'You'll never know how much. Did the letter say anything else?'

'No,' answered Della without hesitation. 'Nothing.'

'Donovan sounded absolutely sure?' asked Dawlish.

'Yes.'

'Did you tell anyone else about these trail marks?'

'Not for a long time.'

'Why not?'

'I didn't want anyone to follow him,' Della replied. 'If he struck it lucky, he wouldn't want anyone to know about it. It would start a rush and spoil everything. Donovan had said he mustn't tell anyone. It was a postscript, underlined. I can almost see it to this day.'

'Della,' Dawlish said, 'have you still got Donovan's letter?'

'Nigel took it with him.'

'Did Nigel say nothing else about it?'

'Absolutely nothing,' Della assured him.

'Whom did you tell eventually?' asked Dawlish.

'A friend of Nigel's.' Della's reply was almost too casual. 'Jeff Mason, I mean. He went off to look as far as the black hills, but there was no sign of an abandoned Land-Rover or of anyone working. He kept on trying to convince me that Nigel would never come back, and I'm sure he hoped he wouldn't, but when he did come, Jeff was very good.'

'Isn't he the man who came to the rescue on the night you were attacked?'

'Yes,' answered Della. 'He's always at hand to help. Always.' She sat without speaking for several seconds, looking as if into the empty distance.

'You're absolutely sure Nigel didn't utter a word when he got back?' Dawlish insisted.

'Of course he didn't, don't be ridiculous. He was hardly breathing.'

Unbidden, a picture of Felicity's face, of Felicity hardly breathing, came to Dawlish's mind. He shut it out.

'Did he bring anything back?' he asked.

'Nothing,' Della said. 'Absolutely nothing. He had on a shirt and a pair of shorts, an old hat and some palm-frond sandals and belt. There wasn't anything in his pockets. Absolutely nothing. Would you like to see?'

'Very much,' said Dawlish.

She jumped up and went into the bedroom. He followed her to the door and saw her bend down in front of a chest of drawers. She took out a cardboard box and brought it across. She put it on the table and took off the lid. The pathetic little oddments of clothing looked as if they would fall to pieces if they were lifted out.

Dawlish picked up the sandals. They were worn through at the heels and probably would not have lasted for another few days. The belt was in much better condition. He drew it through his hands, the round edges pricking him, and pressed it between his thumb and forefinger. He was not consciously looking for anything; it was almost a reflex action.

In places the belt was flat and limp; in others it was lumpy and hard. Hard. He did not glance at Della but bent the rope over sharply near one of the lumps. The dry palm frond cracked and frayed.

'What are you doing?' Della asked quickly.

Dawlish said, 'Just checking.' He worked the frond to and fro at the fracture he had just made, and it split in two. A small shiny stone popped out and, as he grabbed to save it, fell on to the floor.

CHAPTER X

THE PROMISE

Della said in a tense voice: 'What is it?'

Dawlish bent down. The 'stone' glistened, just beneath Della's chair. He picked it up and held it out to her on the palm of his hand. It looked like a little piece of glass, perhaps a misshapen glass marble.

'It can't be a diamond!'

'It's heavy,' Dawlish said softly. 'For its size it's very heavy.'

Della didn't speak. Her eyes were glittering, and her lips pressed tightly together.

Dawlish held the stone out to her. Her fingers trembled as she took it. He felt along the roughly made belt for another lump, felt one, and broke the dry frond about it. Another stone of about the same size showed among the fragments. He picked it out.

'Another,' breathed Della.

'Several,' Dawlish said.

'I can't believe it.'

Dawlish said, 'It's certainly not a dream.' He stood up, went to a higher table, and began to break the belt into little pieces.

Fragments of frond littered the table, like chaff, and every now and again a stone fell, sharply. He stopped each from falling. He counted them as he went along but could not be sure he had the right number. He put them in a row, one by one, about half an inch apart.

Della began to count.

'One—two—three—four—five—'

Dawlish checked as she went on, her voice hardly audible.

'—ten—eleven—twelve—thirteen—'

That was the moment when he thought he heard a sound. He did not look up but strained his ears to catch a repetition.

Della was still counting.

'—nineteen—twenty—twenty-one—' and in a whisper, *'Twenty-two.'*

'Twenty-two,' agreed Dawlish. There was a lump in his throat.

He did not hear another sound, but a draught was cutting in from the door; he hadn't noticed it before. He pushed the diamonds together in a heap.

'They can't be real,' Della said chokily.

'Of course they could be.'

'Real *diamonds*?'

'They look like uncut diamonds,' Dawlish said. 'I've seen a few in my time.' He was thinking with one half of his mind about the sound and the draught, with the other half about the diamonds. He judged that the smallest was twelve carats or so, the largest perhaps fifteen. Say an average of twelve each; say fifty pounds a carat; say six hundred pounds a stone or fourteen thousand the lot. That was near enough. Fourteen thousand pounds' worth out of a hundred million pounds' worth wasn't a large proportion, but if these were from the big steal . . .

Was there any way of checking?

Della spoke in a low-pitched voice, breaking into his thoughts.

'Major Dawlish.'

He didn't answer.

'Major Dawlish, there's someone listening at the door.'

'Yes, I know,' Dawlish answered in a tone which only just carried to her ears. He picked up the little heap of diamonds. Two of them slipped out of his fingers and one nearly dropped to the floor. He caught it and noticed that one spot about the size of a pinhead showed brightly. Now that he was aware of the bright spot on one he saw it on the others. He put the lot into the job pocket of his trousers; they rattled, just like small marbles. He yawned and stood up, then suddenly spun round and leaped towards the door. It was ajar. He thrust out his foot and crashed it back. A gasp, a stumbling sound, and a clatter like bedlam. The door swung back towards Dawlish, but now he was near enough to push it open.

A man was reeling back against the rail of the stoep.

'It's Jeff!' exclaimed Della.

Dawlish let her push past him as he looked at Jeff Mason. He had heard of the man both from Ma Parkin and from Della and had expected a much older-looking man. Mason was young for his forty-odd years. He was broad-shouldered and solid but not too fat. Blood dribbled from his nose as he straightened up. He glared at Dawlish.

'Who the hell are you?'

'Jeff, are you all right?' Della sounded genuinely anxious.

'No thanks to him if I haven't a broken nose.'

'Do you make a habit of sneaking up and eavesdropping?' Dawlish demanded.

'Where it concerns Della Forrest—yes, I do. If I hadn't she would be dead by now. Della, who is this big lout?'

As he finished, his eyes widened as if in recognition. Before the girl could answer or Dawlish say anything, he exclaimed: 'You're Dawlish! The English policeman!'

'How many other policeman do you know by sight?' asked Dawlish, putting an edge to his voice.

'Anyone who's seen yesterday's *Star* or *Argus* would have a job not to recognise you,' Mason said. 'Your photograph's plastered over them. What are you doing here? God! Diamonds!'

'That's right.'

'And you found diamonds in those old clothes.'

'You certainly heard me say so.'

'Good God!' exclaimed Mason. 'If I'd had my way I'd have burned the rags. Diamonds—didn't you say twenty-two, Della?' He was dabbing at his nose as he spoke, using a grubby khaki handkerchief.

'You've good ears,' said Dawlish, watching him closely. 'About fourteen thousand pounds' worth.'

'It doesn't make sense. Nigel wouldn't—' Mason broke off, gave his nose a final dab, and went on, 'He said he was going to get diamonds, didn't he?'

After a long pause Della said, 'No one seems to think he might have made a strike.'

'He still couldn't sell them for what they're worth in this country,' Mason declared. 'He'd have to hand them over to the big boys.' There was bitterness in his voice, but he went on quickly: 'Can I see them?'

Dawlish took several of the stones out and showed them on the palm of his right hand. Mason poked at them. Dawlish had a feeling that he might make a grab and run, but Mason finally picked out one stone, weighed it in his hand, then held it in the light and studied it as if with expert knowledge.

'It's real,' he said huskily. 'It's fifteen carats or more. If Nigel made a strike, you're rich, Della.'

'And if Nigel stole them, I'll be alone for the rest of my life,' Della said in a queer little voice.

Mason seemed puzzled as he looked at her. It dawned on Dawlish that this was probably the first time she had given him any inkling of a change in her attitude towards her husband. Dawlish took the diamonds back and put them in his pocket. As they rattled, a car horn sounded some way off.

The black Mercedes was on its way.

'Look here, Dawlish,' Mason said. 'I think I've a right to know what all this is about.'

'I don't know about any right,' Dawlish said. 'But I've no objection to telling you why I'm here.'

By the time he had finished, Bukas had drawn up and was getting out of the car. The sun shimmered on the hard gloss of the top and sides, and somehow the black shininess showed up the yellow-grey drabness of the surrounding countryside. Dawlish found himself narrowing his eyes against the glare, frowning without realising it. It was over-hot, and the light-weight trousers felt like heavy tweeds against his legs.

Bukas came hurrying. He looked almost grotesque behind a pair of sun glasses with huge lenses; they fitted him almost like a pair of goggles. He bowed perfunctorily to Mason and waited.

'Any luck?' Dawlish asked him.

'No one appears to have any idea at all where Mr. Forrest was going. He refused to tell anyone,' Bukas reported. He glanced at Mason, then back to Dawlish, as if wondering whether he was free to talk with this man present.

'We know where he planned to go,' Dawlish said. 'And he came back with these.'

He held out the diamonds.

Bukas was so taken by surprise that he almost tripped over as he moved back. After that startled pause he took off his glasses, examined the diamonds in much the same way that Mason had done, and spoke in a husky voice, as if with disbelief.

'They are some of the jewels we are looking for, Major.'

Dawlish barked, 'Are you sure?'

'These diamonds all have a polished spot of a kind applied only by the Big Star Consolidated for identification purposes.' Bukas paused, 'They are instantly recognisable. I am used to looking for it, but under a magnifying glass anyone could identify such stones.'

He looked at Della almost accusingly.

'Lieutenant, we need to organise a party to go over the ground that Nigel Forrest covered both on his way from here and back to here. Every possible side trail has to be covered too. We will need men who know the southern Kalahari inside out. How soon can it be arranged?'

'If you're going to do it properly, you'll need at least a week,' Mason put in before Bukas could answer. 'And if you've got any sense, you'll take me with you. I know this part of the desert as well as any man alive. I know others who know it pretty well too.'

'Your offer will be noted,' Bukas said coldly. 'Major Dawlish, I recommend that you return to Pretoria while I organise the search party with the help of the police from Buckingham. Meanwhile those diamonds should be taken to the United Diamond Distributors in Kimberley as soon as possible.'

He was so excited that he seemed even younger than before.

'I'll go to Kimberley,' Dawlish said. 'Mrs. Forrest . . .'

'Yes?'

'I think your husband should be taken to the hospital, and I would like to take him with me, for the sake of his own safety. It is obviously possible that he knows a great deal about the missing diamonds, and another attempt to silence him by killing might be successful.'

Della would know there was another motive, too, that in a way this was a form of arrest, of keeping Nigel under observation. Dawlish felt sure that she was acutely aware of that. If she argued, he would have to force the issue, but he did not think she would.

'Where will you take him?' she asked.

'Kimberley.'

'I see.'

'If you would like to accompany him—' began Dawlish.

'No,' she interrupted. 'No, I will stay here. Until I know the truth of what has happened, I will be better off here.'

Della watched them go, Jeff stretched out in the back of the Mercedes. She was not thinking of Jeff, though; she was thinking of Dawlish. He was so big and handsome. He could be so hard and unyielding. For a few minutes while he had been questioning her she had felt furiously angry with him, afterwards all thought of anger had eased from her mind. He had been so gentle, so reassuring, so commanding.

She could see his face clearly in her mind's eye.

Nigel only appeared to her a death's-head.

'Major Dawlish,' Jeff Mason said.

'Yes, Mr. Mason?'

'I don't know what the police have told you, but you'll make a mistake if you don't let me go with that search party.'

'You're very anxious to go,' Dawlish remarked.

'You can say that again! I want to make sure Della Forrest's interests are looked after, but that doesn't alter the fact that I know the desert as well if not better than any man alive.'

'I can believe it,' Dawlish said. 'I'll do what I can.'

'Is that a promise?' Mason was almost as eager as Bukas.

'That's an apt word to use in this case,' Dawlish said. 'I repeat, I'll do what I can. I've no authority in South Africa and could be overruled, you know.'

'If you don't take me, I'll send my story to a newspaper. They'll stake me,' Mason said. 'That's flat.'

'It sounds like a threat,' Dawlish said mildly.

'That's right.' Mason was almost truculent. 'It's meant to be a threat. But I don't want to carry it out. I'd much rather come with you.'

Dawlish smiled faintly.

'We'll sort it out,' he said.

They were at the airfield at Buckingham. Nigel Forrest was already on his way to Kimberley by road, in an old Buick converted into an ambulance. Dawlish was waiting for Bukas, who had been making arrangements with the local police. The more he gave Bukas his head, he believed, the better it would be for the Crime Haters liaison in the future. He had seldom known a more dedicated officer. At odd moments he found himself wondering whether there was any other additional explanation of Bukas's interest in the case, but he did not dwell on the possibility.

Bukas came hurrying, nodded frigidly to Mason, and led the way to the aircraft.

Ten minutes later Dawlish saw Mason vanishing into a tiny dark dot against the grey-yellow land which looked as if it did not know water and did not not know rain. Up here it was blessedly cool. Down there it was like a furnace, and in the heart of the desert it would be far, far worse.

Two hours after leaving Buckingham they approached Kimberley in the full glare of the afternoon light. As they neared the city, Dawlish saw huge grey slag heaps rising out of the ground like man-made mountains. The massive superstructures of the main mines showed up against the sparsely vegetated land. Down there in those few square miles was one of the richest parts of the whole earth.

Soon the aircraft was so low that only the distant buildings could be seen, flat earth very like that near Kangarmie, but broken by many low hills and some scrub. Not far off a muddy river wound its way through tree-lined banks of the bare brown earth.

As the aircraft taxied to a standstill, Dawlish saw Harrison standing near a fire truck with two men, probably United Diamond officials. The sun was shining on his sleek dark hair, and he looked immaculate and cool. Dawlish caught another fleeting glimpse of his similarity to Donovan.

There was an air almost of tension in the three men. As Dawlish approached, and before he was introduced to the other men, Harrison said, 'We have more big trouble.'

Dawlish's thoughts flew to Felicity.

Harrison went on: 'Those marked diamonds are appearing on world markets. Some have been offered in New York, London, Sydney, and Hong Kong. They're rough and uncut, and they're being offered in small parcels at half market price.'

CHAPTER XI

NEED FOR HASTE

Dawlish looked round the horseshoe-shaped table in the board room of the United Diamond Distributors Corporation. It was on the top floor of a tall new building, and from the wide panoramic windows one could see the Big Hole where the fortunes of this city had been founded, and one could see the deep green of the water which filled the depths. On the rim were old buildings, preserved since the days of the early diggers. There were nine men present. The three members of the Crime Haters, Bukas, a Kimberley detective, and diamond-company officials. Each of these represented a big mining corporation, and together they comprised United Distributors, the body which controlled prices and sales for all the South African and some allied mining companies. Outside the room there was the hard bright sunlight; in here there was perfect air conditioning, which made only a faint buzz of sound.

Sir Joel Morpath, Chairman of United Diamond Distributors, was a short, dapper man with a waxed black moustache, a little old-fashioned, obviously modelled on the portrait of the original Joel Morpath which hung on the wall just behind him. Old

Joel had been a contemporary of Cecil Rhodes and the leader of the consolidation of the mines when the digging of the Big Hole had been by spade and pick; murder had been commonplace, and water had been sold at three-and-sixpence a bucket. At all the mines in the district mechanical diggers were shovelling more blue ground in a day than a thousand men had dug in a week in the old days of the 1870's and 1880's.

'Mr. Harrison has told you exactly what is happening and how serious the position is,' said Morpath. 'And he has also agreed that all reasonable security precautions have been taken.'

Harrison nodded. 'Security is reasonable. In fact, it's good,' he said. 'I've visited five mines, seen the vaults and strong rooms, and checked the machinery, much of it remote-controlled. Oh, security is wonderful—to look at,' he added, and then caustically: 'But the diamonds vanished, didn't they?'

'A quite exceptional chain of circumstances must have made it possible,' said Morpath.

'Foolproof security would make an exceptional chain of circumstances impossible,' Harrison retorted. 'The weakness is on the inside.'

'Colonel Van Diesek and other senior officers have checked every member of the staff who might be responsible. Each one has been cleared of all suspicion.'

Morpath touched his moustache; it was already obvious that he had little patience with Harrison, who seemed to specialise in getting under people's skin. That did not make him a bad policeman; an irritant could be a good thing.

'I hope there will be some effort to recover the diamonds and prevent too much harm being done,' Morpath went on icily. 'I have no doubt that the New York and the London police are infinitely superior to ours in the way of crime prevention. That is obviously why the crime statistics in each city are so low.'

Harrison's smile became cheerful and friendly.

'That's a point,' he conceded. 'We ought to put our own house in order first. How about those diamonds, Pat? You've been away for two days. Haven't you found them?'

Dawlish said mildly, 'Not all of them.' He took his right hand out of his pocket and rolled the handful of diamonds along the desk towards Morpath. There was a moment of stupefaction so absolute that it was almost comical. Then suddenly each director snatched at a stone and put it to his eyes. Morpath took a magnifying glass out of his pocket and studied three of them. Harrison stared at Dawlish round-eyed, then leaned towards Van Woelden and spoke in a clear, carrying voice.

'Our Patrick's beginning to convert me.'

Morpath put the three stones down very deliberately.

'These are most certainly ours. I congratulate you warmly, Major.'

'Nice of you,' murmured Dawlish. 'I don't know how far they take us, but . . .'

He made his report briskly and without notes. Morpath took down notes in shorthand; the directors watched Dawlish closely all the time. Van Woelden had a satisfied smile at the corner of his lips. Harrison rocked on the back legs of his chair, to and fro, to and fro. Bukas looked as if he were purring.

'. . . the search party is already being organised at Buckingham,' Dawlish said. 'Lieutenant Bukas can tell us more about this.'

Bukas, quite pallid without his glasses, jumped in vigorously.

"Three Land-Rovers have been hired and are being provisioned for two weeks. I have provisionally arranged for three persons and a driver with each party. The makeup of each is a matter of decision by a higher authority, of course. My recommendation is that the drivers be: *one*, Lieutenant Arvo of the Buckingham depot; *two*, Jacob Parkin of Kangarmie, who knows the Kalahari Desert very well; *three*, a Bantu sergeant also attached to the Buckingham depot who is the best tracker in the area. I am sure he is the best.' Bukas glanced at Dawlish as if to see whether he was going to stake a claim for Jeff Mason, but Dawlish said nothing. 'I also recommend that no one who is unused to the conditions of the desert should take part. At a time of emergency anyone who is suffering from the hardships of the trek might cause much harm.'

Now Bukas looked defiant.

'Meaning me?' asked Harrison lightly.

'The lieutenant is concerned for my old bones,' Van Woelden said. 'Don't worry, Lieutenant. I have no desire to be shaken about in one of your trucks or to sleep on sand which will make me feel I have been bitten by a thousand mosquitoes. There is more than enough for me to do. I will get in touch at once with all the police forces of the cities where the diamonds are appearing on the market. It would help us to take decisive action if we could find all the local distributors.'

Bukas was eager to be generous.

'It is vital, *mijnheer*.'

'Major Dawlish,' said Morpath in a quiet voice, 'I am only now beginning to apprehend the significance of your discovery. For the first time since the theft I feel that there is some reason to hope that we might prevent the damage from becoming too great.' He paused. 'This man Forrest—when can he be questioned?'

'He's at Kimberley Hospital under constant surveillance,' the police lieutenant put in. 'The moment the doctors permit it he will be questioned.'

'And what if he gives information which will be useful to you in the desert?'

'We will be in touch by short-wave radio,' Bukas declared.

'Ah. Yes.' Morpath touched each point of his moustache as if to get inspiration and then went on: 'I understand that this will cost a great deal more than an investigation. My board fully agrees with me that we will meet all the costs. And no expense should be spared, gentlemen. The issues are too grave to take chances.'

'Just what are these issues?' Harrison inquired almost casually.

'I don't understand you.' Morpath was sharp-voiced.

Van Woelden leaned towards Dawlish.

'I have never known anyone like this Harrison. Does he want everyone to hate him?'

'He probably enjoys being an excoriator,' Dawlish said.

'A very serious crime has been committed—' Morpath was saying.

'Oh, sure.' Harrison rocked back on his chair. 'It was a crime and I am a policeman and I will do everything I can to find the criminals. They happen to have murderers on their payroll, and I'm against all murderers.'

Morpath repeated stiffly, 'I don't understand you.'

'I'll make myself very clear,' Harrison said. 'You've been keeping these diamonds on ice. There are plenty more on ice. This way you keep the price of diamonds up. Someone wants to get the price down. This is why they have stolen the cache. This is why they have committed murder. This is why Dawlish's wife is lying in a coma at this moment. Sure, I'm a policeman, and I'd like to know what I'm taking the risks for.'

Bukas said as if outraged, 'A crime has been committed!'

'You're certainly right. If these diamonds had been properly protected, they wouldn't have been stolen in the first place. I am a delegate to the Crime Conference, the Conference you turn to when you're in big trouble. The Conference has two purposes—correct me if I'm wrong, *mijnheer*. These purposes are to solve crimes and to prevent crimes. The best way to prevent crimes is to remove the cause of them. If a cause is artificial, like this one, isn't the cause to blame?'

One of the diamond directors asked hotly, 'Is this a meeting of a morality council?'

'I do not associate myself with Mr. Harrison,' Van Woelden said with great precision.

Dawlish found everyone looking at him, as if for the deciding vote. He gave a half-amused smile.

'I must confess I'd rather like to hear the other side of the argument.'

'There is no excuse for such an attitude as Captain Harrison's— no excuse at all.' Bukas sounded hopping mad.

Dawlish was looking at Morpath, who was smoothing his moustache with his forefinger.

'This attitude is most unexpected from a highly placed policeman, I must say.' He paused. 'But perhaps understandable. Be patient with us, Mr. Harrison. We are not quite so advanced in our anti-monopoly laws as the United States is said to be. However, two factors seem to me indisputable. In the first place, even if the diamonds were half, a quarter, or even a tenth of their value, it would still be a theft. The thieves would still have no right to them. The task of the police is to find the criminals and also the diamonds they stole. Will you concede to that?'

Harrison gave a funny little one-sided smile.

'Conceded,' he said.

'Thank you. The second issue is not so straightforward. However, there are some simple aspects of it.' Morpath went on slowly and deliberately. 'There is a stable world value for diamonds. They are a world-wide trading commodity, which always hold their value, and they make one of the very few steady world price values. In some ways the diamond standard, as it might be called, is as important as the gold standard. Many millions of people have an investment in diamonds. Tens of thousands of retailers and wholesalers throughout the world have large stocks of them. If the market were to be undermined and the value sharply reduced, all of these people would suffer, some of them would be ruined. Moreover, once the price was reduced, faith in them as stable commodity would be gone. Believe it or not, diamonds are a stabilising factor in the economy of some countries—particularly South Africa, the Rhodesias, and South America. Take this stabilising factor away and yet another gilt-edged security will be gone. There are other, more personal or emotional issues. Every woman with a diamond ring, every woman with a diamond brooch, earrings, or pendant—each of these will be robbed. And most of these will suffer far more than the Big Star Consolidated or any of the board. So will the mine-workers. We employ fifteen thousand workers, mostly Africans, in excellent living and working conditions. If we have sharply to reduce the value of the diamonds, we would have to reduce our labour force at once. The margin of profit even at today's prices is not as high as you probably think. There may be something basically wrong in the creation of a form of monopolistic price ring, but it exists, and any variation in prices must be extremely marginal if it is not to be extremely harmful. Do you think people should starve because of the arbitrary application of someone else's principles, Captain Harrison?'

Harrison was no longer rocking back on his chair. He had not taken his eyes off Morpath, who now rested both hands on the table, palms downward, and waited for the American to speak.

'Sir Joel,' he said, 'they could use you in Washington. And if I could vote for you, I would. Thank you, sir.'

A faint smile played about Morpath's lips.

'You are very generous. Now shall we adjourn for lunch, gentlemen?'

It was a simple lunch, the main course beautifully cooked steak, and all perfectly served by white-clad men who moved like shadows.

Immediately after it Morpath called Dawlish aside. Dawlish half expected some reference to Harrison, but the chairman said: 'I had occasion to talk to our London agents this morning, Major Dawlish, and took the opportunity of inquiring about your wife.' Dawlish felt cold fingers gripping him. 'I am told that there is a noticeable improvement,' Morpath went on.

'Ah.' Dawlish felt tension oozing out of him. 'Thank you very much.'

'All thanks are due to you, not only for what you found in Kangarmie, but also for coming here in person.' Unexpectedly Morpath shook hands. 'Is there anything I can do to help?'

'One thing,' Dawlish said thoughtfully.

'Just name it.'

'I would like a man named Mason on the desert search. I don't think the South African police are happy about the idea.'

Morpath raised his eyebrows.

'And you don't feel that you can insist?'

'I don't want to give anyone cause for offence,' Dawlish said dryly. 'I don't mind how much offence you cause.'

After a pause Morpath smiled.

'I think we must both go to Washington together. I'm sure Harrison would vote for you too.'

When Dawlish, Harrison, Bukas, and three Kimberley police reached Kangarmie two days later, Jeff Mason was assigned to one of the trucks as a guide. Dawlish did not inquire how it had been arranged, but Bukas seemed quite amenable. By then the trucks were provisioned and ready for an early start next morning.

Jacob Parkin was the obvious leader.

He was a massive man, not quite so tall as Dawlish, but with a heavier figure. He had a long thrusting jaw, a face turned red by long exposure to the sun and the heat-laden wind. He was nearly bald, a fact often disguised by an old pith helmet, once white, now grey, torn badly and soiled by finger marks both back and front. He wore it on the back of his head most of the time, so that his thick neck was always in shadow. His movements had the stealth quite common to many big men, and his manner was the exact opposite of Ma's, whom he left so often and for such long periods. She was garrulous, hearty, almost too cheerful. He was so quiet-voiced and spoke so seldom that he might be called taciturn. The calmness and intelligence of his grey eyes saved him. He seemed always to be looking into long distances—and even in repose there was a gleam as of anticipation and expectancy in them.

Dawlish had a feeling that Jacob Parkin was a giant among minnows.

In Kangarmie the whole population gathered to see the three trucks off. Even old Mrs. Cratton was steered into a kind of wheel chair, her only means of locomotion, and pushed down to the store. Ma Parkin, her sons and daughters and sons-in-law and daughters-in-law, with their brood, stood, sat, squatted, or sucked as they watched the convoy. Three of the brood sat on the two derelict petrol pumps, one marked S . . . r . . . ll and the other not marked at all; only the newly painted one was left free.

Ma was at the front, back, and sides of them, as if to make sure that none was hurt. Jeff Mason's old father was there, crippled with arthritis, silvery-haired, wizened of face. The wives and daughters, sons and husbands were all there—seventy-one people in all came from the eleven houses, including the Ellises, the Longfellows, the du Toits, and the Browns. Three were away prospecting, and three, including Parkin and Mason, were going with the trucks.

All the servants of Kangarmie were gathered in the shade of the garage next to the store; smiling Basuto and Zulu girls a long, long way from home, boys who had stayed on and found work here after the mines had closed.

Della was not there. Dawlish looked for her and knew that Mason was puzzled by her absence, too, but the search party was virtually on its way. As they passed within two hundred yards of the Forrests' house, Mason stared as if willing Della to appear.

She did not.

Nigel was beginning to feel, to think, and to realise that he was alive. The doctors would not allow any questioning yet, but the word came through every day.

Felicity was improving, very slowly. She still slept, and there was still danger, but it was no longer acute. Temple checked each day and wondered what would happen if she woke and wanted Dawlish.

CHAPTER XII

THE MINES

Dawlish had never known heat like it.

It struck at the roof and sides of the covered Land-Rover, which cast no shadow, for the sun was directly overhead. A long way off a second truck looked like a dark spot against the sandy, rock-strewn earth which the sun had robbed of colour.

They had been travelling for four hours, and Dawlish doubted if they had made fifteen miles.

Behind them was the hill and the mine superstructure, but it was hidden by the rising land behind them. Sand and rocks made straight driving impossible. There was a kind of road, but it was filled with big boulders and deep sand. Half a dozen times they had been forced to stop and dig the wheels out of the sand, and one truck was at least two hours behind. Only four-wheel-drive vehicles could possibly make it. Until that morning Dawlish had been puzzled by the decision to stock up for so long a period to cover a few hundred miles. Now he understood.

Mason was with him, and the truck was driven by the Buckingham policeman, Lieutenant Arvo. Dawlish sat in the front, Mason behind. Dawlish heard him fidgeting from time to time, then suddenly felt a tap on his shoulder. The driver was muttering under his breath, for just ahead was a deep crevice in some flat rock.

'Have to go back half a mile,' he complained.

'Major.' That was Mason, whispering.

'Yes?'

'That crack wasn't there last time I came this way.'

'Are you sure?'

'Major,' Mason said, 'this road's been changed.'

The driver caught the words.

'You crazy, man?'

'That crevice wasn't there before. Half these rocks have been shifted. There was a twenty-mile straight stretch you could always travel by sundown.'

'Are you saying these rocks have been moved here?'

'Rolled, dragged, or trucked, I'm telling you someone's been working on it.' Mason was leaning over the back of the seat; the driver had just put the gear into neutral and was twisting round in his seat. Dawlish saw the sweat creasing his eyes like oil.

'When did you last come along here?' asked Dawlish.

Arvo said reluctantly, 'Six months ago, when I came to arrest the two Africans who escaped from the working party on the road outside Buckingham.'

'I was here two weeks ago,' Mason said. 'It was okay then.'

'How could you shift rocks like these?' Dawlish demanded. 'Unless they used a bulldozer.'

'They could have used one at that.'

'If they had, we would see the tracks.'

'No, we wouldn't see any tracks,' Mason rasped. 'There's a wind every night strong enough to blow the sand about and obliterate all the marks. If you knew this desert you'd know that.'

He wiped his wet forehead. 'I wouldn't like to swear I could find the right road.'

'Let's get down,' Dawlish said.

Arvo stopped the engine. He was a short, stocky man with a brick-red face and very prominent eyes. He got down one side, Dawlish on the other. The sun seemed to burn through the bush hat he wore—an old one lent by the Kimberley police. He wore a pair of khaki drill shorts run up quickly by an Indian tailor, a bush shirt borrowed from the biggest man in Kimberley. It was roomy round the chest but baggy at the waist and short at the rump. He wore long socks and ankle-length boots bought off the shelf. He led the way carefully over the rocks. There was a patch of them, quite dark, spread over an area of half a mile. Beyond in every direction was the desert. The other truck was now out of sight.

Dawlish reached the crevice. It wasn't deep, no more than three feet or so, but the truck couldn't possibly cross it.

'The rock went over here,' the driver insisted.

'Ever have rockfalls here?'

'I've never heard of any.'

'Look,' said Arvo, pointing. 'There's a piece of dynamite casing.'

Halfway down the crevice was a piece of pale-pink paper or board. It was just out of reach. Dawlish started down the rocks and slipped.

There was no danger, but to steady himself he touched sunbronzed rock. He snatched his hand away, it was so hot.

'Careful!' Mason called.

Dawlish waved acknowledgment and went down another foot. He could reach the piece of paper, which was cartridge paper with a marked curve to it. Arvo was right. Just below, out of sight from above, were other pieces of dynamite containers, blown here by the wind. He did not trouble to get these; the one piece was all the evidence he needed. He climbed back and handed it to Mason.

'See that?'

'My God, I'm right!' the driver exclaimed.

'I've been puzzled all the way along,' Mason said. 'I just couldn't understand the road.'

'How long will it delay us?' Dawlish asked.

Mason said thoughtfully: 'It depends how thoroughly it's been done. We can't go far to the south—the valley is impassable to all vehicles. There are sand dunes north and north-west, quite impassable. This road follows the only safe course for wheeled vehicles, the only proven hard ground.' He moistened his lips. 'I wonder if the others have realised this yet.'

After a pause the driver said, 'We'll have to turn back, as I said.'

He started the truck up, and turned it round, and drove with almost nervous care. The truck was jolted from side to side. Once it stuck for a few seconds in deep sand, making it look as if they would have to get out and dig. A desperate last effort cleared them.

'There's Bukas' truck,' Mason pointed out.

To Dawlish it was just one of the other trucks, but when they were nearer he saw Bukas by the side of Jacob Parkin and Harrison's face between them. Mason was proving right very often.

As the trucks drew level, Bukas called out, 'We can't get through that way.'

'Nor can we,' Dawlish called back.

'Mr. Parkin says the road indications have been altered.'

Parkin was getting out of his seat. He tipped his topee forward so that it put his heavy features into shadow. Dawlish got out, and the others followed. Parkin ignored the policemen and looked at Mason.

'What do you make of it, Jeff?'

'Someone means to keep us off this road.'

'Road,' Harrison echoed, in a jeering tone.

Parkin looked at him with those farseeing eyes.

'In Kalahari, Mr. Harrison, this is what we call a road. Jeff Mason and I have travelled over it dozens of times.'

'The rocky patch was dynamited,' announced Mason. 'Ask Major Dawlish.'

Harrison echoed, 'Dynamited!'

Dawlish showed them the piece of cartridge paper.

'When we get back that should help us to trace the gun-powder source,' he said. 'What's your considered opinion, Jacob?'

Parkin did not seem to notice the use of his Christian name. He answered slowly: 'In the past few days a lot of labour has been used on this road, Major. There could be only one reason: to make it unusable.'

'Is it unusable?' Dawlish asked quietly.

Parkin took a long time to consider his reply.

'So they don't mean to let us use this trail,' Harrison said.

'Could they do all this in three days?' Bukas demanded.

Parkin was still considering.

'They could have had a week. They could have been working on it since Nigel Forrest came back.' Mason was crisp and authoritative in all things to do with the desert. 'They might have expected him to send a party back and started work as soon as he got away.'

'Or after the attempt to murder him failed,' Dawlish suggested.

Parkin spoke at last.

'That's right, they could have had a week to work in. You asked me a question, Major,' he went on. 'I think the answer is no—they haven't made the road unusable. But they have made it very difficult to get through. There are two places where they could stop wheeled or track vehicles and send us a long way round.'

'How far round?'

'Eighty or ninety miles. Say two days.'

'Do you agree, Jeff?' Dawlish asked Mason.

'With every word.'

'So we go on for some distance and then decide whether to go the long way round or to go on foot. Is that it?'

'That's right, Major.'

'Just one question,' Harrison demurred.

'Later, Wade,' Dawlish said. 'I don't want to roast out here.'

'I just want to know where the other truck is.'

'It went ahead,' said Parkin.

'How did a truck with a black driver make it if ours couldn't?'

'Don't underestimate the Bantu,' Parkin advised. 'Even behind a wheel some of them can smell out the firm ground. We will follow his tracks for a while and make up some time.'

'Why didn't we do that before?' Harrison asked acidly.

'I want to know what you're insinuating.' It could not take much to make Mason angry.

'Don't get your dander up, Jeff,' Parkin soothed. 'You don't want to worry about a stranger who's just plain ignorant of the conditions. I'll explain to Mr. Harrison as we go. You tell the major.'

He turned and climbed back into the truck.

Harrison's dark eyes seemed to glow with sombre amusement as he looked at Dawlish before following Parkin. Mason muttered, 'Bloody Yank,' under his breath and he turned away. Bukas had stood by, saying nothing, but he was glowering at Harrison. Arvo had been looking at the under-carriage of the truck and poking about at the engine. He was ready as soon as the others.

When Dawlish sat back, he broke out into a sweat which enclosed him with oven heat. For five minutes his head swam and there were little streaks and spots of light in front of his eyes. He wiped the back of his neck, which was runny with sweat. He would get used to this, but until he did he must be very careful with the sun.

'Did you take salt tablets this morning?' Jeff Mason asked.

'Yes.'

'Feeling okay?'

'I'm all right,' Dawlish said. 'What did Jacob mean?'

Mason snorted.

'It was time someone put Harrison in his place! Did you have to bring him along?'

'That wasn't my question.'

'Oh, all right. Trust policemen to stick together. Jacob talked good sense, that's all. There is a long wide stretch of hard land here—it stretches for miles. Here and there it is dangerous where shallow valleys are filled with sand, but at this distance from Kangarmie there are half a dozen places where you can get through. The African driver took a different way from us. I guess he saw that the regular road didn't look so good, so he veered off in the northwest. He'll be at Big Rocks before us. Won't he, Lieutenant?'

'Maybe he will,' Arvo conceded.

He drove a hundred yards or more behind Parkin, who kept twisting and turning his wheel and sometimes crawled at no more than five miles an hour. There was still no sign of the third truck, but Dawlish did not worry about that; there was no need to think about them—Parkin and Mason had every confidence in the driver. It was too hot to think. A long time ago Dawlish had known heat like it, but not for a long, long time. A picture of Nigel Forrest kept coming into his mind. If the man had walked across this desert in this heat, without food or water, it was a miracle he was still alive. The ordeal must have been as agonising as torture.

Would he ever recover properly? Would his mind be unhurt?

Would Felicity recover?

Forrest—Felicity. Donovan. Murder. Sir Joel Morpath with his quiet, reasoning voice. Mason, so often angry. Harrison, for ever asking questions. All of these seemed to merge into Dawlish's mind until it was difficult to distinguish one from another. It was like being in an oven. No, not an oven, a brick kiln. How long were they supposed to keep this up without another rest?

They stopped twice for a sandwich and a drink straight from the icebox. After each stop Dawlish felt much more himself. This was one of those patches which came in every case—the exasperating waiting period. The only difference from normal was the heat. He kept looking for the Black Rocks but could only see the unending sand and scrub. Sand, sand, sand, dirty-looking yellow-grey sand. Here and there huge rocks appeared, great round boulders which seemed to have dropped out of the sky; there was no other obvious way in which they could have come.

At last a great mound of the black rocks appeared in a mass together, making a hill which looked as big as a mountain against this featureless plain. The sun was to the north-west of these and bathed one side in a golden glory. The sight made Dawlish catch his breath, for the impact was even greater because the brilliance put the other side into a pitch-blackness which seemed almost sinister.

As they drew nearer, Parkin's truck stopped on the dark side of the rock. Dawlish watched him, Bukas, and Harrison moving about and then saw them stand in front of a rock, as if reading a notice. When the second truck drew level, Dawlish got out and stretched his legs and arms. It was unexpectedly cool in the dark shade; the savage heat of the day had gone.

'The other truck's gone ahead,' Parkin said in greeting. 'They reckoned they could reach another patch of rocks by nightfall.' He pointed to a message chalked on one of the big rocks. 'We haven't a chance, so we'll camp here.'

They took the provisions out of the trucks, so that two could sleep in each and one sleep underneath. Arvo and Jeff Mason began to get a fire going from desert driftwood in a fireplace made of loose stones. One word they used kept puzzling Dawlish.

Parkin laughed.

'*Brei-vlees* is our word for barbecue,' he explained.

'Now I'm a much happier man,' Dawlish said.

'In half an hour steaks will be sizzling and you'll be fed better than you would in any hotel.' He was erecting a canvas wash-stand and filling it. 'Hot or cold?' he asked.

Dawlish asked without thinking, 'Is it worth heating water?'

'You just leave it on the side of the truck in a tin container, and that's all the heat you want. Evaporating water bags keep the drinking water cool.' He splashed warm water into the washbowl.

The wash was almost as good as a shower.

Dawlish moved about the camping site as the sun went down and the only light was from the glowing charcoal fire. Steaks sizzled, making him realise how hungry he was. The heat of the day was almost forgotten as the cool of evening spread. The stars filled the skies with cold light, and only the sound of men's voices and occasional rustle of movement disturbed the quiet. For once Harrison had nothing disruptive to say.

'We'll bed down around nine,' Parkin said. 'We have to be up around four.'

'I can't get to bed soon enough,' Harrison declared. He climbed into his truck and seemed to put his head down at once. Arvo and Bukas went to bed early, too, but Dawlish did not feel particularly sleepy. Parkin was wakeful too. He lit a pipe, and the rich smell of the tobacco was like a heavy scent on the night air. Dawlish smoked cigarette after cigarette as they sat in silence on upturned cases.

They had not spoken for fully five minutes when Dawlish heard a rustle of sound from the truck behind him. Parkin turned his head. Dawlish had no thought of anything unusual, was lulled into a kind of pleasant stupor.

Parkin's hand fell on his knee, but the big man did not speak. Dawlish watched more intently.

A pair of legs appeared at the end of the truck; someone was getting out feet first and very slowly. Bukas and Harrison were in that truck, but this wasn't either man.

The feet touched the sand. A moment later they saw that it was a small figure—a woman's.

Very softly Parkin called, 'You need a drink and some food, don't you, Della?'

CHAPTER XIII

STOWAWAY

The only light was from the stars and the embers of the fire, but Dawlish was as sure as Parkin that this was Della Forrest. He watched as the girl gave a start of surprise; for a moment it looked as if she might try to run away, but she came slowly towards them. Parkin was already opening the lid of the icebox.

'Come and sit down.' He patted a rock between him and Dawlish, then poured cold tea tinkling into a glass.

Della took the glass as she drew close to him. She looked at Dawlish as if not certain who he was. She seemed dazed and a little stupid. The light was not good enough to see properly, but Dawlish could imagine her pallor. She began to sip, very slowly. Parkin took sandwiches out of the box—they were rapped in cellophane and would keep fresh for days.

'You must have had a hard ride,' Parkin remarked.

'It wasn't very comfortable, but I dozed a lot.' Della's voice was remote and distant.

'Not very comfortable, eh? You hear that, Major. She dozed a lot.' After a pause Parkin went on, 'Where did you ride?'

'In the sample box,' Della answered. 'I had an air cushion. It wasn't so bad.'

'Good a place as any,' Parkin approved. 'Good thing there were holes in it. We drill holes in the rock-sample boxes in case we bring back a snake or an animal,' he explained to Dawlish. In fact, he was giving the girl time to recover from what must have been a great ordeal. 'The box is always empty on the outward journey. You make a habit of riding in one, Della?'

'It's the first time,' Della said. She seemed to speak more clearly, as if the drink had refreshed her.

'You could have chosen a better time to come along for the ride,' Parkin remarked.

'Why did you come?' asked Dawlish directly.

She didn't answer.

'Don't be stubborn, Della,' Parkin reproved gently. 'The major wants an answer, you know.'

After a pause Della said: 'I couldn't wait any longer. I just couldn't wait. I seem to have been sitting and waiting, sitting and waiting all my life. You were going to see where Nigel had been, and I had to find out.'

'Why?' asked Parkin, quite casually.

Della said sharply, 'Major Dawlish knows why.'

'Does he, then?' Eyes turned towards Dawlish in the darkness. 'That so, Major?'

'The way things look, Nigel might be a thief,' Dawlish answered. 'Della told me when I first came that she had to know whether he was or not.'

The answer seemed to satisfy Parkin.

'You had a long wait all right,' he said. 'Another week or two wouldn't have made any difference, though.' After a pause he added shrewdly. 'I suppose you felt better when you knew what you were waiting for.'

She didn't answer.

'Question is, what are we doing to do with you?' Parkin said musingly.

'I'm coming with you.'

'We'll have to think about that,' said Parkin. 'You want another sandwich?'

'Oh, please.'

'We'll have a talk in the morning.'

'Then you'd better get some sleep,' the big man said.

It was barely daylight when they struck camp, but before they set out Dawlish saw the canvas sacking and inflated air pillow in the big box in the Land-Rover where the girl had been all day. It must have been unbearable in there. He had a suspicion that Jacob Parkin had not really been surprised to find her but had suspected where she was.

Jeff Mason seemed stupefied when he learned, Bukas angry.

'It would be a grave mistake to take her further,' he declared. 'There is shade here. We can leave food and water for her and pick her up when we come back.'

'Even a cold-blooded policeman wouldn't do that,' Mason said.

'It is her responsibility. We are not called upon to increase risks and the difficulties because of an impetuous young woman.'

Dawlish found everyone looking at him, as if at a judge.

'I'd say we could use a cook,' he said.

Mason was grateful and relieved. The girl looked across at him with a grateful little smile, as if she had expected nothing less. She did no more than her share in packing up, in an atmosphere which Bukas made unpleasant by his stiff disapproval.

Harrison said to Dawlish, 'If our Afrikaner friend goes on like this, he'll take my place as the odious boy of the party.'

'I'd like that,' Dawlish said dryly.

Harrison laughed.

They drove towards the pale morning sky line with the sun rising behind them. It was a strange, clear light, which placed beauty on the rocks and the sand, the tiny scrub and the gentle undulations of the earth.

They drove very slowly but without so many obstacles as on the day before. Mason kept pointing to objects familiar to him, rocks of unusual shapes, skeletons of big game driven down here by occasional storms, wrecks of old tyres which the sand had made into strange circular earthworks. Dawlish was amazed by the positiveness of each identification, as well as by the slowness of the journey. They passed another, smaller group of rocks by midday, stopped for half an hour in its shade, then crawled across the desert towards the second major objective— the baobab tree. As they sat, thrown this way and that by the unending bumps, he tried to picture two things: Nigel Forrest, crossing this desert on foot. The small army of men required to change the course of the road.

Where had they come from? The same place as Forrest?

If only Forrest were conscious and could talk or could be made to talk.

There was another question now: why had Della stowed herself away? Had it been an emotional impulse? Why had Parkin said nothing if he had in fact suspected that she was hiding in the truck?

In the middle of the afternoon they heard a deep boom of sound which seemed to come from ahead of them. Arvo slowed down to listen for a repetition, but there was none. Parkin's truck stopped and they caught up with it. Parkin never missed an opportunity to climb down, and he was waiting in the shadow of the truck. Della still sat in it, leaning out of the back.

'Jeff, do you know of anyone blasting around here?' Parkin asked.

'I don't understand that bang either,' Mason said.

'Is there any rock to blast?' Dawlish asked.

'Unless someone's planning to mine fairly deep, no,' answered Parkin. 'Lieutenant, keep in my tracks, will you?'

'What are you expecting?' Harrison asked.

'The unexpected,' retorted Parkin.

'Is there any other section of the road they might wish to alter?' demanded Bukas.

'Shouldn't think so.' Parkin turned away and began to drive even more cautiously. Dawlish sensed a greater anxiety in his mind since the booming sound. Mason sat staring at the girl whose head and shoulders were outlined against the back of the other truck. Harrison, sitting next to Parkin, appeared to be dozing.

Suddenly Mason exclaimed, 'See that smoke?'

He pointed almost straight ahead. Dawlish saw a haze against the sky line. Pale grey, it seemed to move sluggishly, where everywhere else there was stillness. They went on, the tension increasing. The cloud of smoke seemed to become nearer and darker, higher in the sky, yet spreading over a wide area.

The brake light of Parkin's truck went on.

Della disappeared from the back of the truck, and Harrison sat upright. Arvo pulled a little towards one side, so that they could see beyond the first truck.

A man was coming towards them on foot, a black man. Dawlish didn't recognise him but guessed it was the driver of the truck which had gone on ahead. He was limping. As they drew nearer they saw that his left arm hung by his side, dripping blood, and there was an ugly gash at the side of his forehead.

Perhaps a mile behind him the plume of smoke seemed more pale.

Parkin and Bukas were hurrying from the truck; Harrison and Della stood in the shade. The second truck drew up behind as Parkin and Bukas reached the solitary man.

It was the Bantu police sergeant.

His face was drawn with pain, and Dawlish marvelled that anyone so badly injured could have come across that parched, burned land beneath the awful sun. The man spoke to Parkin, who stood still for a moment and stared at the smoke.

'What the hell's happened?' Mason asked roughly.

Bukas, looking like a troglodyte with his huge dark glasses, was doing something to the African's injured arm. Parkin turned, put his hands to his mouth, and roared, 'Pitch a tent, get a fire going, and the first aid ready!'

Della, Arvo, and Harrison put up the tent. Dawlish collected small rocks to build a fireplace, and driftwood—spiky and painful to handle. Arvo opened the Red Cross box at the side of the truck and spread out the antiseptics, bandages, scalpels, and dressings. There was a hypodermic syringe, too; he loaded this from a little bottle of morphine. While all this was going on, Bukas was carrying the injured man and Parkin was hurrying back towards the main group.

As Parkin drew nearer, Arvo called, 'What happened, Jacob?'

'The truck was blown up,' Parkin answered flatly.

It was a moment or two before the significance of that sank in. The truck was blown up.

Dawlish saw Bukas staggering under his load and hurried to help him, not really comprehending the situation. The face of the injured African, twisted in pain, was shiny with sweat.

'Please, be very careful,' Bukas said. He was breathing hard, and sweat was pouring down his face too.

Dawlish sensed the concern in his voice and understood it when he saw the injured man's lacerated arm. He took the man gently, cradling him. Parkin's voice seemed to echo in his ears, *The truck was blown up.*

Bukas was staring straight ahead. 'Ran over a mine,' he announced.

Dawlish echoed stupidly, 'Mine?'

'He was having a rest from driving and was in the back. He was thrown clear.'

'What about the two in the truck?'

Bukas said, 'They were blown to pieces.'

Parkin looked down at the African sergeant, who was lying still in a drugged sleep. He lay on a table made of board over two boxes, and Harrison was cutting away the sleeve of the old jacket he was wearing. Della was near the fire, where a can of water was boiling. No one doubted that the left arm would have to be amputated just beneath the shoulder.

'Need me, Jacob?' Dawlish asked.

'Not right now, Major.'

'Della!' Dawlish said sharply. 'Are you all right?'

'I will be,' she said.

Dawlish, Bukas, and Arvo drove off in the second truck. The evening sun was still scorching; it tinged the thinning smoke with a purple pink colour. Arvo drove in the tracks of the vehicle which had been destroyed. Some of the twisted metal was still red-hot. Two hundred yards or so away was a piece of tyre, a pick, a smashed box of provisions, the cans dented but not broken. A litter of other debris made a trail right up to the wreckage.

There was a man's hand.

There was a box, empty.

There was a burned and blackened torso.

Bukas said in a very low-pitched voice: 'If that was placed to stop the truck, there will be other mines to stop us. They will have laid a row of them. How are we going to get through?'

CHAPTER XIV

THE BAOBAB TREE

Dawlish did not answer Bukas' question.

This scene carried his mind back to North Africa during the war, to burned-out trucks and charred human bodies. In those days it had not been safe to step heavily without clearing the mine field or risking death; he had often had to risk death.

Were there other mines here?

He studied the position of the wreckage. It appeared to be on a kind of slightly higher ground. Some ankle-deep scrub probably bound the sand together to make it easier for the wheels to get a grip. The 'road' seemed to run slightly uphill.

Bukas repeated, 'How are we going to get through?'

'They can't have laid many,' Dawlish said. It was like talking of unbelievable things, and in fact it *was* incredible that such deadly methods should be used.

'They could have laid enough,' Arvo remarked.

He had spoken very little on the journey and was always in the background, a shadowy figure without any personality. Some deep emotion, perhaps hatred, put fire into his eyes.

'We'd better salvage what we can,' Dawlish said.

'First we give these poor devils a burial,' said Arvo. Then a storm of words burst out of him. 'How am I going to tell their wives? They're friends of mine, been friends for years. How am I going to tell their wives?'

'I don't think you've ever sheered away from a job you had to do,' Dawlish said.

'We'll go together,' Bukas said huskily. 'I've known—'

He broke off, choking, looking into Arvo's eyes; two big men hardened by their years in the police, could hardly see each other for unshed tears. Then Arvo swung round and grabbed a spade.

The digging took half an hour. By the time it was done Parkin and all the others appeared. Again Dawlish was reminded vividly of North Africa: a shallow grave, a murmured valediction, a wooden cross made of wood from a box. The mood of disbelief remained.

They turned their backs on the grave, salvaged food, the first-aid box, and a few tools, and drove back to the tent where the injured man lay, still unconscious from the drug.

'What do you plan to do now, Major?' Parkin always deferred to Dawlish.

'We've got to get that man to hospital, but we don't want to lose another truck,' Dawlish said. 'We ought to radio for a helicopter. It should be here at first light, and we can get him loaded and lose very little time.'

'We can send Mrs. Forrest back, too,' Bukas said.

Della didn't speak.

'Will you call Kimberley?' Parkin asked Bukas.

'Immediately.' Bukas jumped up and went to the radio, glad of something to do. The others watched him climb into the back of the truck, with Arvo just behind him.

'Major,' Harrison said, with that half-mocking note in his

voice, 'did you expect to find yourself involved in a military operation?'

'No, I certainly didn't. But with a hundred million pounds at stake it shouldn't really surprise us. Is there an army depot near Kimberley?'

'Yes,' said Mason. 'Why?'

'We could use a couple of mine detectors too.'

'I'll go and tell Bukas.' Mason jumped up, glanced at Della, and went off at the double. Della was sitting on a box, staring towards the wreckage.

'They certainly mean to make sure we don't get through,' Parkin said. 'If they'll go this far, they won't stop at anything.'

'They couldn't expect to hold the police off for ever,' Harrison reasoned. 'They must be playing for time. Can anyone guess what they want to do with it?'

'They want to get rid of something,' Parkin said.

'Like diamonds, maybe?'

'I'm wondering what trouble Bukas is having in getting Kimberley on the radio,' Dawlish said.

A moment after he had spoken, Arvo jumped down from the truck. Almost at once Bukas followed him. Both policemen spoke to Mason. As they all came towards the others, Parkin said in a shocked voice: 'There's more trouble. It shows in their faces.'

'They can't work the damned thing,' Harrison said, shaken out of any hint of pose.

Bukas called: 'All the transistors have been smashed. We cannot send word through.'

Dawlish felt a cold shiver run through him and sensed the others felt the same; it was like a chill wind in the desert, setting their nerves tingling. Della moved towards Dawlish. Bukas took off his glasses and his eyes seemed to glare as if he were looking for the culprit here.

Dawlish said, 'Someone has to take Sampson back to hospital.'

No one spoke, so no one argued. All knew it was the inescapable truth, but no one wanted to go.

'Major Dawlish,' Bukas said at last, 'I was ordered to take your instructions.'

'Over to you, Major,' Parkin said, poker-faced.

'I'm not going back,' Mason declared as if he expected to be told he would have to. 'I don't take orders from anyone.'

'Two will have to go,' Dawlish said flatly. 'Lieutenant Arvo.'

Arvo simply nodded his head as if expecting to be named.

Dawlish looked at Harrison. 'Sorry, Wade.'

Arvo closed his eyes, as if suddenly realising the task which had drawn much nearer, of telling two women how their men had died.

Harrison opened his lips as if to protest, his expression giving away his surprise and his impulse of refusal.

He said, 'You've forgotten something, Major.'

'What have I forgotten?'

'One of us here damaged that radio.'

'Not necessarily.'

'Then who else?'

'It could have been damaged before we left.'

'You don't believe that,' Harrison half jeered.

'It doesn't matter what I believe,' Dawlish said. 'Don't make it more difficult for me.'

'There's still the thing you've forgotten.'

'Haven't you told us that yet?'

'No sir. You've forgotten that if I go back with a police lieutenant, that leaves you and Bukas alone with the chief suspects.'

Mason said angrily, 'Are you suggesting I damaged that radio?'

Harrison looked round at each one of them in turn and spoke with great deliberation: 'You, Jeff, or Jacob, or Della, maybe. Not a policeman, that's for sure. So it had to be one of you three.'

'That's a reasonable argument,' Parkin conceded matter-of-factly. 'So you ought to send us all back, Major. Then you won't have anyone except Arvo who knows the desert, and he doesn't know it very well. He hasn't been across here for six months, and the desert changes a lot in six months. So what do you propose?'

Dawlish looked at Harrison, smiling faintly.

'Wade, I want you to go back with Arvo and Sampson. I know you don't have to and I can't make you, but I'm sure it's the best way.'

'Convince me,' Harrison invited.

If two policemen go back together, you'll certainly get through. If I sent one of the others with one policeman, you might not get all the way back.' 'You could send Arvo and Bukas.'

'I can't go on without a South African policeman with me, and you know it,' Dawlish said. 'You and I are here by their courtesy.'

Harrison echoed, 'Courtesy!' He laughed explosively, but the expression in his eyes was nasty. Then, to Dawlish's surprise, he said: 'I'll be back with a helicopter. Don't make any mistake, Dawlish. One of the people you're landed with smashed those transistors and that means they are hand in glove with whoever blew up that truck.' He looked at Parkin and Mason with cold accusation, but neither man spoke. Then he said to Della, 'If it's you sweetheart, I will personally cut your throat.'

Parkin said to Dawlish, 'Do you think Harrison's right, Major?'

He was standing with Dawlish and Mason by the side of the truck, at first light next morning, their third day. Della was securing one of the tins of water, only a few yards away from them. Bukas was checking the engine and the usual levels.

'He could be,' Dawlish said.

'That makes odds against you.'

Dawlish said lightly: 'Three to two? I've known a lot worse.'

'This is all nonsense,' Mason put in roughly. 'If the major suspected one of us, he wouldn't come along with us.'

'I don't think you know the major,' Parkin said dryly. 'When he says he's had worse odds, you can be sure he's telling the truth. You finished, Della?'

She called, 'Half a minute.'

'Lieutenant?' Dawlish called.

'I am all ready.' The hood went down with a bang.

'Jacob, don't you forget our chief problem is getting through without being blown to pieces.'

'I no longer think there is any such danger,' Bukas declared. He came across, pulling off a pair of oil-blackened cotton gloves. 'If this truck is blown up, all of us go with it.'

'I almost wish I was on the other side, I hate your guts so much,' Mason said.

'No doubt you do,' Bukas retorted.

'Take is easy, Jeff,' Parkin said. 'The lieutenant is simply saying that he hopes you and I are not working for the thieves. If we aren't, we might be blown to pieces. If we are, we won't. That right, Major?'

'There's another problem,' Dawlish said, as if it had just occurred to him.

'What is it?'

'Five people in one truck.'

'There's plenty of room,' Parkin said. 'Do you want me to drive?'

'Will you?'

'Glad to.' Parkin sounded as if he meant it.

He was smiling to himself as he started off. Bukas sat beside him; Della and Dawlish were in the cushioned seats on the back, and Jeff Mason was on the rock box with a blanket folded over it. Parkin drove carefully but not with the extreme caution of the previous day. It would be easy to feel that he now felt free from danger. Dawlish kept on seeing the wreckage of the other truck in his mind's eye.

Della began to doze. Mason, his moustache looking more bristly than ever, could not keep his eyes off her. She lolled sideways against Dawlish, and Mason seemed to long to change places with him. For greater comfort Dawlish slid his arm round her shoulder. It reminded him vividly of the way she had clung to him in the paroxysm of tears back at her home.

At last Mason picked up a book of cartoons and began to look through it.

'Major,' Della whispered in Dawlish's ear.

He started.

'Can you hear me?'

'Yes.'

'I didn't damage that radio.'

'That's good.'

'I'm serious.'

'I'm sure you are.'

'I know who did.'

Dawlish pressed her shoulder gently. Mason was turning the pages of the book. The rattling of the truck probably stopped him from hearing the whispering.

'Who was it?' Dawlish asked.

'Jeff.'

'Did you see him?'

'No, but—'

'Why do you hate Jeff?' Dawlish asked.

'I don't hate anyone.'

'Then why do you accuse him if you're only guessing?'

'I heard him.'

'When?'

'When I was in the box.'

Dawlish began to wonder if she could possibly be right. She had been in that box for a whole day. Mason had been in the back of the truck most of the time, and the radio transmitter was next to him.

'How do you know it was him?'

'I could hear him.'

'What makes him so easy to distinguish from anyone else?'

'Listen to him,' she said. 'Listen.'

She stopped. Dawlish strained his ears to catch the sound she wanted him to hear. Above the noises of the truck, at regular intervals, there was a faint, a very faint, whistling sound. It was the way Mason was breathing. Once he was aware of it, Dawlish seemed to hear nothing else.

'Hear it?' Della asked. 'He whistles as he breathes.'

'But I was in the truck all the time!'

'You were in the front of the truck and there was a lot of noise. Major, I tell you it was Jeff.'

There was no way of being sure she was telling the truth. She herself might have damaged the radio and be blaming Mason; certainly she had had plenty of opportunity. But if she was telling the truth Mason was their man, or one of them.

'Major,' Della whispered again.

'Yes?'

'Be very careful.'

'I'll be careful.' After a pause Dawlish went on: 'We'll have a chance to talk about it later.'

'All right,' Della said.

She seemed to fall asleep a few minutes later and seemed completely relaxed, as if she felt quite safe with the protection of his big frame. Where she leaned against him Dawlish felt very hot, but he did not try to make her shift her position.

They stopped twice for food and drink. Dawlish moved to the front, with Parkin at the wheel. Towards evening the baobab tree showed suddenly and unexpectedly against the skyline. As they drew nearer, its huge trunk looked black and solid, but the thin branches at the top, bare of leaves, seemed to have been taken from a much smaller tree and grafted on. In the slanting rays of the sun the trunk cast a long black shadow. Parkin pulled into this and Dawlish stepped into the welcome coolness.

The first thing he saw was a big heap of ashes in a fireplace which had obviously been there for a long time. Yet it had been used recently, probably by a group of men. Della and Mason prepared the meal. Parkin and Dawlish put up the tent while Bukas began his interminable fiddling with the engine, wearing the oily gloves.

After the meal Dawlish strolled away from the big tree. It was dark, but he heard Della following and guessed that Mason wasn't far away. But if he kept his voice down, Mason wouldn't hear him.

'You said you wanted to talk,' Della said. She stood close to him, and their bodies almost touched.

'Yes,' Dawlish said. 'If you think it was Jeff, you're in the best position to find out what he's doing and why they're so anxious to stop us from going on, aren't you?'

CHAPTER XV

ALLEY

'I don't understand you,' Della said. 'How can I find out what is in Jeff Mason's mind?'

'He's eating his heart out for you, isn't he?' Dawlish asked.

After a pause Della took his arm and clutched it.

'I hope you don't mean what I think you mean.'

'I most certainly do.'

'Make up to Jeff?'

'Is is so impossible?'

She took her hand away.

'It's the last thing I'd expect you to suggest.' Her eyes seemed to flash indignantly in the starlight.

Dawlish chuckled.

'Don't fool yourself, Della. Someone tried to kill Nigel. Someone tried to kill you.' He paused, with a flash of recollection that hours had passed since he had thought of Felicity; that seemed almost a blasphemy. The tone of his voice changed. 'A man was murdered in London, two men slaughtered in cold blood here, and Sampson—'

Della interrupted, sounding almost humble.

'I see what you mean. I'm sorry I was such a prig.'

'Della.'

'Yes.'

'Nigel is the only man you have known, isn't he?'

After a pause Della responded softly. 'Yes. He's the only man in my life. But you know how I feel today and how I hate myself for feeling like it?'

'I do.' Dawlish pressed her arm. 'I think you could find out how you really feel, deep down, and at the same time find out whether Jeff is involved in these crimes.'

Della said painfully, 'You mean, if I let him make love to me, I'll know whether I've really gone cold towards Nigel?'

Dawlish didn't answer at once. He shouldn't be surprised by her simplicity, and yet in a way he was. How old was she? The question was in his mind hardly before it was on his lips.

'Twenty-three,' she said without hesitation. 'I was married to Nigel when I was seventeen.' Her voice seemed to float away on the velvet night. '*Sev-en-teeeeen. . . .*'

So she had been married six years, over two of which had been spent in that period of loneliness and waiting. She had fallen in love and married—and to this day it seemed to her wrong even to think of another man. He wondered what he would think if she were his daughter; the one, the only, thing missing in his life and Felicity's was children.

'I'll try,' she said suddenly.

'Della, don't take this too . . .' He paused, searching for the right word. 'Too solemnly. It won't do you or Jeff or Nigel any harm to encourage Jeff a little.'

'But if he thinks I'm yielding, he may take advantage of it.'

Dawlish wondered what kind of books she read and then remembered there had been very few books in her home.

'He won't go too far,' Dawlish said. 'He'll be afraid to spoil his chances.'

'But he hasn't a chance with me! Whatever happened to Nigel, I couldn't think of—'

'Hush!' Dawlish urged.

She fell silent. The night was still; nothing at all stirred nearby. He doubted whether her voice would have carried to anyone, but men used to the desert developed remarkable faculties, and Mason spent much of his life out here.

Della took his hand, holding it very tightly.

'Major—'

'My name is Pat.'

After a pause she went on, 'I won't know what to ask him.'

'Wait for him to talk. If he promises you—'

He broke off as Della caught her breath. He remembered vividly what she had told him, that Nigel had left her with a promise of diamonds on his lips. With a thoughtless cruelty he was telling her that if Jeff Mason promised her great gifts, it might be because of the fortune he believed was his.

Dawlish squeezed her hands very gently.

'I'm sorry, my dear.'

'If he promises me diamonds, it will be because he's a thief,' Della said stiffly.

'It's possible, no more than that. Just let him talk.'

'What makes you sure he will talk?' Della demanded. Her mind was working again now. She had recovered from her first conventional reaction and also from the hurt.

'He's very lonely, Della,' Dawlish reminded her. 'He has no one to talk to. All he's been doing for years is waiting for you.' He felt her shiver.

'I see,' she said. And after a pause she went on: 'I'll try, but—' She seemed to grope for the right words.

'Yes, Della?' Dawlish encouraged.

'You won't let him—' she broke off.

'If you want me, just call out,' Dawlish said. 'One call will be enough.' He felt her hand slide out of his and was tempted to ask why she felt so sure that Jeff might overreach himself. But she seemed to have withdrawn herself as well as her hand.

When they got back to the tent, Parkin and Mason were playing two-handed poker. Bukas had a torch shining like an enormous glow-worm into the engine of the Land-Rover. Mason eyed Dawlish and Della as they came up with a hint of suspicion in his eyes.

'You want some beer?' asked Parkin. 'I could do with a wet.'

'I could, too,' Mason said. He dropped his cards and jumped up.

'I'm tired,' Della said. 'I'll go to bed.'

'If Ma knew you were here, she'd towse you,' remarked Parkin.

It all appeared to be so quiet, normal, natural. The stars seemed too close to the earth and the ground was soft to touch. The clinking sounds of the beer cans, the *clunk* as Mason opened them, were so commonplace that any thought of danger seemed remote. But when Dawlish sat by Parkin's side, while Bukas still tinkered, Parkin said, 'Still feel someone is going to cut your throat?'

'I still think someone might try.'

'Play strip poker?' inquired Parkin.

'Not tonight.'

The big man gave a soft laugh.

'What was Della talking about?'

'Her fears.'

'I've known her for six years, and she never talked to me about her fears. Nor to Ma.'

'It's easier to tell a stranger that you're afraid your husband might be a criminal.'

'Correct me if I'm wrong, but I thought Forrest was a

victim?' Sarcasm wasn't Parkin's strong point, and it sounded laboured.

'That's right,' said Dawlish. 'Why should anyone want to kill him if it isn't to make sure he doesn't talk?'

Parkin ruminated: 'So she thinks her Nigel was involved in the thefts, does she? Do you?'

'It's one of the things I'm trying to find out.'

'Yes, you would,' Parkin said reflectively. 'You're certainly a good trier, Major.' After a pause he went on, 'Can you sleep with one eye open?'

'One eye, one ear.'

'Because if you're right about Jeff and me, you might be wrong about Lieutenant Bukas.'

'That's right,' Dawlish said. 'Jacob, may I tell you something?'

'Ugh?'

'I don't scare easily.'

'I've noticed that,' Jacob Parkin said. 'I didn't think I was going to, Major, but I've taken a liking to you. Let me tell you something. This is my land. This and all this part of the desert—it's my land. I share it with the others who've spent most of their lives here. I don't begrudge them a share of it— they've earned their share. Nigel Forrest, Jeff Mason, old Ma Cratton, everyone in Kangarmie. Anyone who is prepared to give up years to try to wring a fortune out of this Godforsaken hell of a desert deserves anything he gets. Most of them die. My father died. My brother died. It broke their bodies and it broke their hearts. The legacy they left me was the desert to work in until I die—or until I find the fortune they died looking for.'

His low-pitched voice stopped. There was passion and feeling in the words but little in the way they were uttered. He tapped out his pipe on a rock and began to fill it. Only the starlight shone faintly in his eyes, but Dawlish had the feeling that they were seeing far off.

'I want to know I'm not on your side,' Parkin went on very quietly.

Dawlish said, 'Those who are not for me are against me.'

'Fair enough,' Parkin conceded. 'I want you to know that all I've ever believed in puts me on the other side, that's all. I wish they hadn't committed murder. I hope they get caught and punished for that part of it—those who are responsible for that part of it, anyhow. Not the others, understand?'

'You know them, do you?' Dawlish murmured softly.

'I know there are a lot of them,' said Parkin. 'And I know they feel as I feel. They've lived all their lives under the cold-blooded injustice of it all.'

'Injustice,' echoed Dawlish, simply to provoke him.

The calm eyes turned towards him and held steady.

'That's the only word that fits, Major. A man buys land, or he inherits it. He works it and finds diamonds or he finds gold. So he has to sell it to the United Diamonds or the gold companies, the people you saw at Kimberley. The robbers.'

'Sir Joel Morpath, a robber?' Dawlish asked without any feeling.

'In a manner of speaking, yes,' Parkin said. 'Morpath owns too much. He controls too much. He fixes the price any prospector can sell at. I'll tell you something you probably don't know, Major. Between here and the Skeleton Coast there is blue earth so close to the surface you can scrape up diamonds in your fingers. U.D.D. keeps a sea patrol and an air patrol going over those areas. If you pick up a single diamond without turning it in at the price it pleases U.D.D. to pay for it, God help you.'

Dawlish said, 'I wish Wade Harrison were here.'

'Where does he come into it?'

'He liked Morpath too.'

After a long second Parkin laughed on a soft note.

'You're the most honest man I've met,' he said. 'Or the most guileful.'

'I was thinking the same thing about you,' Dawlish said amiably. 'Jacob, you may have a case. I don't know whether you have or not. I'm very glad I'm not here to pass judgment. All I want is a killer. I've come a long way to get him. I'm here with the approval of your police, remember, and you're acting for them. So if you're an honest citizen, you're after the killer too.'

'I'm on their side,' repeated Parkin. At last he lit his pipe. 'I just want you to know that if we do catch up with them, I don't know what I'll do. I don't make any promises. I told the police I would drive you whenever you wanted to go in the desert. Now I'm telling you that if you ever get there you might never get back. If I was in your position, an Englishman out here in a country he knows nothing about, I'd go home as soon as I could.'

'Would you, Jacob?'

'I'd say it was none of my business and go home.'

'But it is my business,' Dawlish objected. 'It's what I'm paid to do, and I've a personal involvement. I can't go home until the job's finished.'

Parkin drew deeply on his pipe until it glowed brightly, showing the tip of his nose a pale red, and putting a baleful glow into his eyes.

'I'll tell you one thing more,' he said. 'I wish I didn't have to take you any further. And I'll tell you another. I haven't got any time for Bukas. He's so set in all his ideas he couldn't bend over to save his life.'

'He tells me he's bending over double his average to avenge Van Diesek.'

'If you want to believe that, believe it.' Parkin stood up, peering towards the darkness where some small boulders were black even against the light. 'What do you think Della and Jeff are up to?'

Dawlish said, 'Is it my business?'

Parkin laughed.

'If you didn't put her up to it, I'll be surprised. I hope you know what you're doing.'

Dawlish said, 'You can't blame Della if she feels lonely.'

'I don't blame Della for anything,' interrupted Parkin. 'But I know Jeff Mason. He's been standing by, waiting for her, for a long time. It didn't do him any good. He never was a naturally patient man, and he's held himself in so tight that when he explodes he'll explode. I don't want Della to be in the middle of the explosion.'

It would be easy to say that Della was old enough to look after herself, and Dawlish was tempted; he did not. In truth, he wasn't sure. If she needed help, just call, he had said, but a hand over her mouth would stop her from calling out.

'Mason isn't a beast,' he said.

'Tantalise them enough, and all men are beasts,' said Parkin.

Della could feel Jeff's arm at her waist. He was quivering, not trembling, but quivering as if her nearness and the very touch of the warmth of her body were exciting him beyond endurance. They were near the spot where Dawlish had been with Della. The rocks were strewn about freely here, and for the past ten minutes they had talked constrainedly, always groping for words. Jeff's voice had a high, dry note. Della felt the same kind of constraint and a kind of revulsion; it was the only word for it. At times recently she had felt warmly towards Jeff, but always when he was at a distance.

They had talked about the awful death of the two policemen and of the injured Bantu driver, in jerky little sentences.

'You were wonderful, Della, when Jacob amputated his arm.'

'Someone had to help.'

'I didn't like to see you there. I didn't think you'd stand the sight of blood.'

'I nearly fainted.'

'You certainly did not!'

All the time Jeff had edged nearer. Then he had put his hand at her waist, and now they were sitting thigh to thigh.

'Della.'

'Yes?'

'What was Major Dawlish saying to you?'

'Nothing much.'

'You like him, don't you?'

'He's all right.'

'You were with him a long time.'

'Oh, don't be silly!'

'But you were. If Nigel had known, he would have wondered what you were up to.'

'Well, he didn't know and never will.'

'Della, I—I didn't expect Nigel to come back.'

'I always knew he would.'

'Now that he's back do you feel the same about him?'

She sensed that this was the critical moment, that if she could say the right thing now she might spur him into making a confidence which could help Dawlish, could help to solve this awful problem. She did not know what to say, but out of her deep simplicity the right words came.

'He is like a stranger,' she said. 'I can't help it, in fact I hate it, but he seems like a stranger.'

Jeff's arm tightened about her waist. She could not be sure

whether it was accident or design, but he raised his hand a little, a very little. She could feel his breath against her cheeks and his heart pounding.

'Della,' he said. 'Listen to me. Please listen to me.'

CHAPTER XVI

THE OLD MINE

It was a simple fact that Della had never sat with another man like this. In those young and carefree days before she had met Nigel she had not been greatly interested in boys, certainly not enough to let them touch and caress her. There was the strangeness of the moment added to a sense of guilt and a sense of mission, all warring within her.

'Nigel's not right for you,' Jeff said in that quivering voice. 'He's a nice chap, but he's not right for you. Anyone who would go off like he did, time and time again, shouldn't be married. Not when he's young. You're much too good for him. He's always neglected you, don't you realise that?'

A few days ago she would have slapped his face for saying such things and would have defended Nigel fiercely, fought for him if need be. But the spirit had been subdued in her, and she did not feel anger; rather did she feel a sickening sense that Jeff was right.

'I hate to stand by and watch you wasting your time on him,' Jeff went on doggedly. 'It's criminal, that's the only word for it. Della, listen to me. I love you. I can't think about anything or anybody else. You're all I care about, all I want. I'm not like Nigel. I won't promise you the earth, but I won't leave you stuck on your own week after week, either. I can get a job in any mine, diamond or gold—I'm a damned good engineer and they're short of engineers. We're the salt of the earth. Come away with me. Don't go back to Nigel. Come with me to Kimberley or Jo'burg or Welkom—I had a big job offered me at Welkom a few weeks ago. It's the coming place. It's got everything—modern shops, picture theatres, the lot. Let me take you away from Kangarmie. You'll never regret it. I swear you'll never regret it.'

Della sat absolutely still, astonished by what he said. She had felt so sure that Dawlish was right. She was equally astonished because in these few moments when she should have hated this man she felt warmer towards him than she ever had before.

She realised then that she wanted above all else to get away from Kangarmie. In a confused way, too, she began to feel that she wanted to get away from her past.

Jeff's arm was very tight about her.

'Don't give me your answer now, Della. Think about it. If you'll only make yourself think, you'll realise what a hell of a time Nigel's given you.'

He took his arm away. He was still quivering and his voice shook. She felt a sense almost of shame that she had been frightened of him.

It wasn't difficult to speak to Dawlish next morning, not too difficult to tell him as much as he needed to know. Della had slept well that night and knew that she looked her best. The others were packing the Land-Rover. Dawlish and Della were putting out the morning's breakfast fire.

'So he didn't promise you the earth,' Dawlish mused.

'Or diamonds,' Della said.

'But he did break the radio.'

'I'm sure he did.'

'Still absolutely sure?' insisted Dawlish.

'It couldn't have been anyone else. I noticed how his breath whistles even when he was talking to me last night. I think it's when he breathes through his nose. Major—'

'Pat.'

Unexpectedly and firmly she said: 'It's no use, I can't call you Pat. I much prefer Major.'

'Then Major it shall be,' said Dawlish almost humbly. 'All right, Della. Thank you very much for trying.'

'Has it helped at all?'

'It might help a lot in the long run,' Dawlish encouraged her, Across his words there came a shout from Parkin.

'You two going to be all day?'

It was the hottest day they had experienced so far. None of them said an unnecessary word or stirred an inch more than he had to during the afternoon. The air seemed too hot to breathe. Everything outside the truck was so hot that one snatched one's hand away at the touch. They did not stop more than ten minutes at any one time, for the heat rising out of the sand seemed to burn the soles of their feet through the thick boots or shoes. Nothing seemed to matter until late in the afternoon, when the sun shot its arrows of heat treacherously from the near horizon.

'There's the mine,' Parkin said. 'We've made it.'

A great man-made mountain rose against the sky. the steel work, the steel ropes, the huge buckets in which the gold ore had been carried to the crushing plant and then to the washing plant were still there, metal ghosts of a dangerous past. The sun glistened on the pale mountain. Here and there in its slopes tiny specks glinted as if they were gold.

Near the entrance to the mine was a huge open shed, once used for a car park. As they drove into it, twenty degrees seemed to drop off the temperature in a few seconds. At one end of the shed were doors, and over one door was the word *Shower*.

'That's a bad joke,' Dawlish said hoarsely. Stiffly he strode to the door. What he wanted most was to find out if anyone had been here recently, but it was hard to concentrate on that. The word 'shower' conjured up such visions of cascading water, coolness on his hot body.

He reached the doorway and stopped. Yet again something almost incredible thrust itself at him, something that seemed unreal. In the midst of this heat and desolation, the dryness and the dreary derelict mine workings, there was a pool of water.

He stepped inside the shower room. There were a dozen shower cubicles. Three of them were damp, had certainly been used in the past few hours. One whole day in this heat would have dried the water up.

Bukas appeared behind him.

'See that?' Dawlish said, fighting to curb his excitement. Someone had been here recently; part of this place was in running order. His heart began to thump. What else would they find? What else was near? Acute awareness of danger, stifled by the heat during this horrible day, began to fill his mind with new issues, new urgent problems.

'Water!' exclaimed Della. 'Look!'

'So the water pump's been working,' Dawlish said, still hoarsely. 'Now we're probably in trouble. Keep close to me.'

'They won't dare to attack us now,' Bukas scoffed.

'Won't they?'

'Major.'

'Yes?'

'Do you still think Parkin and Mason are on our side?'

'I'm still not sure.'

'I have a suggestion to make.'

'Go ahead.'

'Immobilise them,' urged Bukas with great intensity. 'Lock them up in one room here so that we can search the mines by ourselves.'

'We would still have to get them back,' Dawlish pointed out.

'Your friend Harrison should soon be here,' Bukas argued. 'By morning the danger will be much less.'

'Let me think about it,' Dawlish temporised.

Bukas' eyes glinted almost angrily as he said: 'What is there to think about? We cannot trust them all and we don't know which one we can trust. If we lock them all in one room, we will be quite safe.'

'Except from anyone who might be around here,' Dawlish said dryly.

'At least we would not fear there was danger of a knife in our backs.'

'Let me think about it, will you?' Dawlish insisted. He turned to the light switch on the wooden wall and pressed it down. Light came on; light and water were in daily use here although the mine was supposed to be derelict.

'Major,' Bukas said, 'one other thing you must know about. If you want to use the Land-Rover, push the self-starter to the right first. I have adjusted it so that if it is operated in the usual way it will—it will not work.'

Dawlish eyed him thoughtfully.

'So you think they might try to leave us standing here?'

'If they do, they'll never get away,' Bukas said with curious intensity.

Dawlish would have pressed his questions but heard footsteps outside. Bukas must have heard too. He drew back.

'A lot of people must have been here,' he said.

'A hell of a lot.' Parkin spoke from the doorway. 'Major, we've found plenty to tell us who worked on that road. Come with me, will you?'

Dawlish and Bukas followed him, Bukas' expression one of acute suspicion. Once his glance at Dawlish seemed to say, 'Well, you can't say I didn't warn you.'

On the other side of the big shed, hidden at first by the wall of a building, were six bulldozers and four other tractor vehicles. In the big corrugated-iron workshops there were tools and spare parts, cans of engine oil, a petrol pump—all in working order. The sticky odour of oil lay heavy on the air. It was obvious that a sizeable working party had been here until a day or so ago at the latest.

As they went out, Parkin pressed a switch; almost at once an engine began to throb.

'The water pump,' Parkin said.

'You seem familiar with the place,' Dawlish remarked.

'When it was still a gold mine, I worked here for six years.'

Dawlish didn't speak.

Della and Mason appeared in a doorway, Della flushed and almost excited.

'Come over here!' she called. 'The kitchen is stacked with food.'

It was a large, square kitchen, once used for cooking for two or three dozen men. Two refrigerators, with old, worn tops, stood against one wall; one was working, the other empty. Stocks of frozen foods filled a sizeable deep-freeze cabinet. Canned goods and provisions of various kinds were in the other refrigerators and in cupboards.

Della was by a huge sink.

'Major!'

'Yes, Della?'

'There are *nine* cups and saucers, nine dinner plates—nine of everything.'

'Nine of them,' Parkin said. 'And four of us.'

Della didn't protest at being left out.

Bukas said: 'Is there anyone here? Have you seen anyone?'

'I've seen no one,' Parkin answered flatly.

'They've cleared out,' said Mason. 'We've scared them away.'

'It is obvious that they cannot have gone far,' Bukas said. His eyes seemed pale and enormous without his sunglasses, and he looked more tired than any of the others. 'We must have a guard over the Land-Rover all night.'

'Is that what you think, Major?' Parkin asked.

Dawlish said briskly, 'I think we should have a look round while it is still light, then have a shower and a good tuck-in, then stay in one room together until morning.' He glanced at Bukas, who seemed satisfied with the compromise. 'Let's get moving,' Dawlish urged.

'In a group?'

'Yes.'

Parkin looked amused.

No one looked amused when they stepped inside a small engineering shop near the mine shaft, once a maintenance shop for the mine. Some of the heavy lathes and stamping presses were still there. A narrow bench ranged along one side. There were six stools in front of the bench, six tiny lathes in front of each stool, and all the tools needed for diamond cutting and polishing. All over the benches was a powdering of dust—shimmering white, like powdery crystals. It was diamond dust. On the bench were a few uncut diamonds, left about as heedlessly as if they had been pebbles off a beach.

Dawlish picked one up. A tiny point of light glimmered in it.

'These are all U.D.D. stones,' Parkin said softly.

'They have all been here, and that can only mean one thing,' Bukas declared hoarsely. 'They can't be far away. They can't be.'

'That's reasonable,' Parkin conceded. He was standing very still, with a stone in his hand. 'There are fifty thousand rands' worth of diamonds here,' he went on. 'More than I've ever seen in my life. More than I've ever seen in my whole life.'

His eyes seemed to be reflecting the long weary years of his past.

'There are more here than Nigel had,' Della said chokily. 'He must—he must have been working here.' She stood with a little heap of diamonds in her hand, then suddenly flung them to one side. As they clattered about the wall and the floor, she rushed towards the door and outside. Mason went after her as if he dare not let her out of his sight.

'Trouble with Jeff, he won't even learn there are times not to talk to a woman,' Parkin said. 'This seems as good a time as any to set things right, Major.' As he spoke he opened the drawer in the bench and took something out. It wasn't until he pointed it at Dawlish and Bukas that he revealed what it was: a gun. It was like the one which the man Donovan had used on Van Diesek, small, stubby, ugly. 'Don't get excited Lieutenant. It won't help. If you do what you're told, you won't get hurt. Nor will you, Major.'

He smiled faintly.

'I knew it!' cried Bukas. 'I knew—'

He started forward. A spark glinted in Parkin's eyes, and he cocked the gun. Dawlish shouldered Bukas to one side and he went staggering. When he fetched up against the wall he was livid with rage.

'You're a wise man, Major,' Parkin said. 'This gun's loaded.'

'You should have let me—' Bukas could hardly get the words out.

'Kill yourself,' Parkin finished for him. 'Is death so attractive?'

'You murdering thief—'

Parkin shook his head.

'Not a murderer yet, Lieutenant. Not me. But I can't let you and the major do what I know you'd want to do—go after the others with the main load of diamonds. Nothing would stop you, Major, I know that. I just couldn't take a chance.'

'I'll kill you one day!' Bukas almost screeched.

'What's your big complaint?' demanded Parkin. 'What makes you hate the way you do?' He glanced at Dawlish. 'Don't edge nearer, Major. I don't want to operate on another casualty.'

'You cold-blooded swine!' Bukas was absolutely beside himself. 'You killed Van Diesek. You killed—'

'No, Lieutenant. That was Donovan. I never did like Donovan and I wouldn't have allowed him to go to London if I'd been able to stop him. He was our contact man in Pretoria, and I was out here. I couldn't stop him. I knew he was a killer, but he wasn't under my orders. I'm no killer.'

'Your friends blew up that truck,' Bukas accused.

Parkin actually sounded sad. 'You can't blame me for a crime committed without my knowledge, can you, Major?'

'No, Jacob, you can't.'

'You're a fair-minded man, which is more than I can say for the lieutenant. I'll tell you another thing, though. That wasn't murder. We broke up the road in a hurry and used some old land mines left here after the war. There was a desert-warfare training ground near Kangarmie. A lot of old mines were left in the sand. No one meant to blow that first truck to pieces—we just didn't clear that area well enough.'

Dawlish said, 'You might have trouble proving that, Jacob.'

'I daresay you're right. But then—'

Parkin broke off. There seemed no sound outside, nothing to

alarm him, but he stayed on the alert until Della's voice became audible, although it was impossible to hear what she was saying. A note of excitement sounded in her voice; that was all.

Parkin relaxed.

'Just stand quiet,' he ordered. 'If you do, you won't get hurt.'

Almost as he finished, Bukas shouted: 'Mason! Della! Keep away, keep away!'

Parkin glanced swiftly towards the door. Dawlish was too far away to stop Bukas from moving. He leaped at Parkin, who simply shifted his gun and shot him down. On the instant Dawlish moved. There might not be another chance like it; he must take the chance which Bukas had made with blind courage. He reached Parkin as the big man swivelled the gun round. He chopped his right hand down into Parkin's wrist, and the gun dropped. He kicked it out of reach as Parkin came for him. Parkin was the older man by ten or fifteen years, but he was as powerful as anyone Dawlish knew. If he had any or special skills, he might be impossible to beat.

Outside Della and Mason came running.

Inside Bukas lay still.

Parkin brought his knee up towards Dawlish's groin in the old fighting trick, the way of the man who relied on his strength rather than his skills. Dawlish half turned, took the bony knee by the thigh, snatched at Parkin's outflung arm, and jerked him to one side. Parkin thudded against the wall, banged his head, and struggled to stop himself from sliding down the wall. Dawlish swung towards the gun on the floor, but before he reached it Mason spoke from the door.

'Don't touch it, Major.'

He also had a gun.

CHAPTER XVII

THREE TO ONE

'Jeff!' gasped Della. 'Jeff!'

She was just behind him, peering over his shoulder, but Mason took no notice of her. Dawlish, half crouching, stretched out for Parkin's gun. He twisted round so as to see Mason, whose right hand was quite steady. Parkin was shaking his head, as if that way he could rid himself of pain.

'Jeff!' cried Della.

She might give Dawlish the split second he needed, distracting Mason before Parkin was in the fight again. She pulled Mason's shoulder. He thrust his left arm behind him and held her off.

Dawlish started to move. There was a second sharp crack of sound, and a bullet struck the floor between his outstretched hand and the gun.

'Don't do it Major,' Parkin called painfully. 'Don't make us kill you.'

Dawlish straightened up.

'Jeff, you must be mad!' Della was gasping for breath.

'I'm not mad,' Mason said. 'Della, please don't interfere. I'll work it all right if you don't interfere.' There was pleading in his voice. 'Go away for ten minutes. Just go away.'

'You're mad!'

'I'm not mad,' Mason said desperately. He did not look away from or lower the gun from Dawlish. 'This is a man's job. You'll never regret pretending you didn't see a thing.'

Della stood gasping as if appalled.

'Listen, Della,' Mason went on in an appealing voice. 'I meant everything I said last night about how I feel. But this is a different kind of job and I'm in it up to my neck. Just keep out, Della.'

'You told me you'd get a job. You lied to me!'

'You were friendly with Dawlish, and I knew what he was after,' Mason said. 'We had to get him here as he'd got this far. Can't you see that? I can't back out now. I can't.'

He gave the impression that it was agonising to have to reason with her but he had no choice of action. Even if it cost him any chance with her, he would have to see this through.

'Jeff,' Dawlish said quietly, 'here is your chance to back out and make amends. If you do the right thing now, I'll make sure you don't suffer for anything you may have done in the past. This is your one chance.'

Mason was sweating.

'Jeff—Jeff, please . . .' Della began.

'Jacob,' Mason forced himself to say, 'go and get your gun. Hurry.'

Parkin moved across and picked up his gun. There were red veins in his eyes, as if he were suffering a lot of pain, and his face was pale, but there was a smile at his lips.

'Good boy, You keep Della out of it, Jeff,' he said.

He turned towards Bukas, hesitated, then brushed his hand over his forehead. He did not bend down over the stricken detective but said to Dawlish, 'See how he is.'

'I know how he is,' Dawlish said icily. 'He's dead.'

'Make sure.'

'Do your own filthy work.'

Parkin's face went very pale, and his eyes seemed to become a deeper red. He raised his voice for the first time in Dawlish's hearing.

'Do what I tell you, Major.'

It was the wrong issue to force. It went against the grain to obey, but it was the wise thing, Dawlish moved across and went down on one knee over Bukas. He wasn't absolutely sure that the policeman was dead, but the instantaneous impact of the bullet made it seem likely. So did his stillness.

He felt the man's pulse and could feel nothing.

He turned him on one side, very gently, and saw blood on the floor and a big patch on his shirt. And gently he placed Bukas back as he had been. Then he straightened his legs and arms.

'Oh, God, he's dead, he's dead!' Della cried. She was by Mason's side, utterly appalled by what she saw.

Mason put his gun away.

Parkin said, 'He jumped me, Major.'

'That's right,' Dawlish said.

'I wouldn't have shot to kill.'

'Wouldn't you?'

Sweat was like raindrops on Parkin's forehead.

'No. I wouldn't. You know it.'

'It's murder,' Della said in a high-pitched voice. 'It's murder.'

Parkin still looked at Dawlish and for the first time he did not give the impression that he was looking into the distance. There was appeal in his eyes, perhaps also fear.

Dawlish said, 'When you play with fire, you get burned.' He turned to Mason. 'So you did smash the radio.'

'So what?'

'So that you could give your accomplices time to get away,' Dawlish said. 'They won't get far.'

'They'll get far enough.'

Dawlish spread his hands.

'They won't,' he said. 'Nor will you two. No man can get away from his own conscience. You've killed and you've aided and abetted killing. You'll live with it, no matter how long you live. You may be as wealthy as Croesus, but you won't get away from the haunting. The only respite you'll ever get is when the police catch up with you. A lot of murderers have told me that. They're happier when they're caught than when they're supposed to be at liberty.'

'You talk too much,' Mason said harshly. His breath whistled loudly through his nostrils.

'And you will get caught,' Dawlish went on with a tone of absolute certainty. 'It always works out that way. Every police force in the world will be after you. You haven't a chance of escape.'

'Jacob,' Mason said thickly, 'shut him up.'

'Let him talk,' Parkin argued. 'What he says doesn't make any difference. We know we'll get away with everything.' He looked squarely into Dawlish's eyes. 'The only thing I hope is that you don't make us kill you, Major. I don't want that to happen.'

Dawlish said bleakly, 'You didn't want Bukas to die, did you?'

'Shut him up!' shouted Mason. 'If you don't, I will!'

His gun came out again.

'No!' Della cried. 'No, don't. Don't shoot Major Dawlish.'

All the restraint which Mason had imposed on himself broke. He glared at her, body tensed as if he would strike her.

'You and your bloody major! That's all I ever hear, all you ever talk about. Major, Major, Major! You care a damned sight more for him than you ever did for Nigel. My God, when I think of the way you've held me off and the way you butter him up! Major, Major, Major! I hate his guts!'

He was glaring at Della.

She looked at him quite steadily, her expression slowly hardened. She did not speak when he had finished but simply turned her back.

'Major,' Parkin said, 'there's a little room by the showers—a maintenance room. I'm going to take you there. You can take what food you want and what drink you want. There's even a shower. Just go quickly and don't force us to make more trouble. You're a sensible man. You know the odds are too heavy. Just go quietly, without any more talk.'

Dawlish said: 'I'll go, but it won't help you. If you leave here, you won't have a chance.'

'Why, you—' began Mason. He looked as if he would use his gun, but as he stepped forward Della flung herself at him, scratched and kicked him, forcing him off his balance, forcing him to turn and fight her off. Parkin covered Dawlish at a safe distance and made no attempt to interfere with the couple as they struggled.

Suddenly Mason struck Della on the face, sending her reeling sideways. He sprang after her, caught her wrist, and twisted her round.

'She'd better cool off, too,' he said harshly. 'Keep her with the bloody major.'

He spoke as if he knew whatever else he had done he had ruined any chance he had ever had with Della Forrest.

'What are we going to do?' Della spoke in a whisper as if afraid that they might be overhead. 'What are *they* going to do?'

Dawlish felt a deep compassion for her, touched with real affection. It was a long time since he had met anyone with such simplicity and such lack of sophistication. Whatever she felt, she said; fear, joy, happiness, misery, grief, shock—all of these reflected on her face like moonlight on the surface of a lake. A red patch on her right cheek, where Mason had struck her, was going to become a bruise. Her hair had been mussed up in that fierce attack on him, and she had only tidied it up with her hands. Her face was shiny and her upper lip beaded with tiny spots of sweat.

They were in a room which had obviously been used years ago as the maintenance engineer's room when on night duty. There was one camp bed, two upright chairs and one easy chair, several tattered old books and magazines and some newspapers. On the table was a pile of food which Dawlish has brought out of the kitchen. The shower room, with a W.C. and hand basin, were opposite the outside door.

'Major, tell me—what are we going to do?'

'For a little while longer we're going to wait,' Dawlish said. 'It won't be long.'

'They're going to kill us.'

'Jeff won't kill you, and Jacob isn't a killer.'

'He murdered Lieutenant Bukas,' Della said slowly.

'In his queer, twisted philosophy he regarded that as self-defence,' Dawlish said.

'But we can't sit here doing nothing, surely. We've got to stop them from getting away. And what about the men they're working with? They're killers, aren't they? Doesn't it mean anything to you that two—no, three policemen have been killed? Don't you care what happens to those devils out there?'

'I care a lot more than you'll ever know,' Dawlish said.

'They're going off and leaving us here, and we may never get away. Don't you realise that?'

'Della,' Dawlish said, 'You've been quite wonderful. Don't spoil it by getting too excited now. Harrison and other police will be here in the morning. Jacob and Jeff know it. There's no point in killing us. Everyone would know. They'd never be able to go back to Kangarmie safely. They've only one course.'

She spoke more composedly. 'I don't understand you.'

'They've got to get away before the police come here tomorrow.'

'You mean they'll drive off tonight?'

'Yes.'

'In the darkness?'

'They know the desert inside out,' Dawlish said. 'They think they can make it.'

They considered this for a few moments, and then there was a sound outside.

'*Listen*,' gasped Della, betraying her taut nerves.

They sat side by side, keeping very still. There was a sound different from anything they had heard that day: the distant throbbing note of an engine. Della jumped up. The throbbing was some distance off and did not muffle other, nearer sounds. There were heavy footsteps outside, and Mason called to someone, 'How long are you going to be?'

'Coming,' Parkin called.

'Leave the rest behind, and get moving.'

'They're escaping,' Della said tensely. 'How can you sit there and do nothing? How can you?'

'It's the hardest job I know,' Dawlish admitted. 'It won't be long.' He tried to restrain her, but she jumped up and ran towards the door in a frenzy and tried the handle, pulled and pushed, kicked and pounded. The door did not budge, although she would have smashed it down. Perhaps that was why she swung round and screamed at him.

'Coward, coward, coward?'

He sat hard-faced, as if listening for some new sound. Della rushed to him. The engine they had just heard was much nearer and louder. The vibrating note shook the walls and the cans of food and the framed prints on the wall.

'You must try to stop them!' screamed Della. 'You must!'

She raised her arms as if to belabour him as she had Mason. He moved suddenly, pinioning her arms and lifting her, dumping her on his knees and holding her so that she could not free herself. She writhed and wriggled, kicked and tried to punch him, but all he did was to hold her fast.

There was a harsh grating sound, of a self-starter being pulled.

'Oh God,' Dawlish said. It was like a groan. 'God forgive me.'

The grating sound came again, and the roaring of the engine seemed right overhead. Della, no longer moving, was gasping for breath. Dawlish could picture the scene outside: Parkin and Mason in the Land-Rover making a desperate attempt to start the engine, the helicopter overhead sweeping the earth with its searchlight.

Eeeeech, the self-starter screeched.

Dawlish was clenching his teeth.

Eee . . .

Suddenly the self-starter sound was lost in a deafening roar. The walls of the little room shook; glass at the windows smashed; a cascade of tins dropped to the floor, thumping and rolling. The explosion seemed to echo and reverberate for a long, long time, and the noise overhead seemed to die away. In fact it was still there. Slowly the nearer echoes faded, but there was a different sound, a roaring. Through cracks in the shutters of the windows there were glimpses of a fire, flames already leaping high.

Della had become absolutely motionless. Dawlish pushed her to the other chair, jumped up and rushed to the door. He crashed his body against it as once he had against the door of his bedroom in London. It gave way. Outside the flames roared from the heart of the truck. Pieces of metal were strewn about. The shambles were worse than that in the desert because of the lurid glow.

Dawlish drew back, knowing there was nothing at all he could do.

'You knew what would happen,' Della whispered.

'Yes, I knew.'

'You told them not to go. You told them they hadn't a chance. You knew.'

Dawlish said, 'Bukas fixed it, Della.'

'*Bukas?*'

'He wired the explosive to the self-starter and added a safety switch,' Dawlish said. 'He told me.'

'That's why you waited,' Della said. 'Oh, dear God, how awful, how awful it all is.'

Low in the sky, its searchlight centring on a spot perhaps fifty yards away, a helicopter was hovering. The pilot was careful to keep well out of the range of the fire. The engine roared louder as it came down. Against the glare of the searchlight Dawlish saw it land and saw men running across the desert towards them. He couldn't be sure but thought Harrison was in the lead.

It was Harrison who appeared near the open doorway first, who saw Dawlish outlined against it, and came running. The lurid light lit up his face and showed his great anxiety, his fear.

'Pat, are you all right?'

'I'm all in one piece, if that's what you mean,' said Dawlish heavily.

'I thought they'd blown you to little pieces,' Harrison said. After a pause he went on, 'Don't tell the world, but I didn't like the idea.' He caught sight of Della. 'Where's everyone else?'

Dawlish answered very slowly. 'There isn't anyone else.'

Harrison did not speak or move. Other men from the helicopter came hurrying, keeping their distance from the fire. Before any of them were near enough to hear, Harrison drew in his breath.

'Then how about the next best thing?' he demanded. 'Where are the diamonds?'

CHAPTER XVIII

MYSTERY REMAINING

In the machine shop there were the uncut stones which Della had hurled away from her, and in one of the drawers there were two cigarette boxes of them, tucked away. The three policemen who had come with Harrison, Harrison himself and Dawlish searched every part of the buildings, every hiding place it was possible to search by night, but found no more diamonds.

Outside the battered maintenance hut and among the debris of the wrecked truck they found dozens more stones strewn about by the explosion.

As he searched, Dawlish talked to Harrison and one of the police from Kimberley, telling the whole story, explaining just what had happened.

By seven o'clock Harrison said: 'We can't do any more until morning. You need sleep nearly as much as Della does.' He grinned. 'You like the needle too?'

'I'll sleep without it,' Dawlish said.

Before he went to one of the bunk beds in a shed which had been used recently by half a dozen men at least he looked in to see Della. She was on a camp bed in a corner of the kitchen.

Harrison had persuaded her to take a sedative injection and she was sleeping soundly, as if quite untroubled.

Harrison joined Dawlish.

'She's just a kid,' he said. 'And I've news for her.'

'What's that?'

'Hubby's coming round. They expected him to be able to talk by tomorrow.'

Dawlish said softly, 'I hope it's good news for her.' They walked away, Harrison looked curiously at Dawlish. No one else was in the bunkhouse. As they undressed, Dawlish said, 'Thanks, Wade.'

'For what?'

'Getting here so fast.'

'You knew I would, Major. You knew nothing would keep me away a minute longer than I had to. Persuading the Kimberley people that it was worth flying by night wasn't the easiest thing in the world, but they're good guys at heart.'

'Bukas was good,' Dawlish said. 'Much better than we allowed.'

'Pat . . .'

'Yes?'

'You carry the troubles of too many people on your shoulders. A man has only so much responsibility.'

'If we're going to moralise, a man has as much responsibility as he is alive to or aware of,' Dawlish said. 'You don't blame a man for being shortsighted; you correct his vision.' He finished stripping, and as he stepped towards one of the blessed showers, Harrison studied his magnificent body with unfeigned admiration. Water hissed and splashed. Harrison went into the next cubicle. After five minutes they started towelling.

'I want to know something,' Harrison said.

'That's a nice change!'

'Why did you let Parkin and Mason kill themselves?'

'They wouldn't listen.'

'They would have listened if you'd told them about the trap.'

Dawlish said stonily, 'Would they?'

'You know they would. And if we'd caught Parkin he would have been the witness we needed. We want those diamonds, remember. Three hundred million dollars' worth.'

'Morpath certainly won you over.' Dawlish spoke in the kind of jeering tone that Harrison so often used.

'You're hedging,' Harrison accused.

Dawlish slipped on his underpants and sat at the side of his bunk.

'Yes, I'm hedging,' he admitted. 'And yes, I could have stopped them if I'd told them what I suspected. I wasn't sure, mind you— Bukas didn't get round to telling me. You might have caught Parkin alive. I doubt it. I think he would have killed himself rather than be caught. He was a very proud man.'

Harrison was looking at Dawlish narrowly but didn't speak.

'He went out quickly, at a time when he thought he might win,' Dawlish went on. 'If he'd been caught and put on trial, he would have gone through hell.'

'You're not that soft-hearted,' Harrison objected. Mason would have talked even if Parkin wouldn't. When you let them die you killed two more witnesses. Vital witnesses.'

'Think so, Wade?'

'You know so.'

'No,' said Dawlish. 'I don't know anything of the kind. We'll find the diamonds.'

'Will we? I'm not so sure.' Harrison let his curiosity get the better of him. 'Think they're down in the mine?'

'No,' Dawlish said. 'Wade, you were right first time. I need some sleep.'

'With this much on your conscience, do you think you'll sleep?' said Harrison, back in his half-jeering mood.

'Good night,' Dawlish said. 'Thanks again.'

When he woke it was broad daylight. He was alone. The heat was already stifling, and he was startled to find it was after eight o'clock. He had a quick shower, put on singlet and slacks, pushed his feet into his shoes, and went outside. No one was about. The wreckage had been cleaned up and all trace of the bodies removed. He scanned the ground but saw no sign of uncut diamonds, so any left in the wreckage had been found. He went beyond these buildings. The helicopter, for all the world like a grotesque giant insect, was two hundred yards away, its bulbous nose shimmering in the sun. Two men were over by the old mine shaft, a hundred yards or so in the other direction, and as Dawlish watched Harrison climbed into sight.

Dawlish heard a sound behind him, turned, and saw Della. She wore a big palm-frond hat, roughly made, and beneath it she looked tiny and fragile.

'Hallo, Della.'

'Good morning, Pat,' she said soberly.

'That's better!'

'I'm sorry I carried on so last night.'

'You'd have been a heartless wench if you hadn't.'

Her eyes smiled, but not for long; in a way she looked more sombre than he had yet seen her.

'I've found something,' she said. 'I've been searching for hours. Will you come and see what it is?'

She was very subdued but gave him no clue to her discovery.

Harrison and the others were still busy. Dawlish went with Della across the baking hot earth into a room which had some benches, darts, a small billiard table, table tennis—everything for a recreation room. In one corner were some small lockers with numbers on them. Della opened Number 7 and took out a bundle of letters. Now tears were brimming over and beginning to fall down her cheeks.

Dawlish looked at the signature of the first letter. It was: *My love for ever and a day, Nigel.* He felt a sudden stab of understanding and did not need to look further. He handed the letters back, and Della said chokingly:

'He wrote something to me every day. *Every* day. He was kept a prisoner here. He didn't want to stay, but they made him. It was Donovan. Donovan brought him here and told him what the work really was—cutting those stolen diamonds. Cut diamonds don't cause so much trouble in South Africa, only uncut ones. Did you know that?' It wasn't really a question, and she did not pause. 'I haven't read all the letters, but Nigel keeps on saying how he wants to get away, how he longs to see me. He wouldn't have anything to do with the crimes at first and wanted to leave, but Donovan and the others were afraid he would tell the police, so they kept him prisoner. He was waiting, as well as I.'

Tears almost choked her.

'All the time I was waiting he was a prisoner here, and—and he wrote every day. Every—'

She turned and ran from Dawlish as if this was a burden she must carry by herself, and Dawlish did not follow her. When her footsteps had faded, he looked inside the locker. There were pencils, a photograph of Della so torn and creased that Forrest must have handled it thousands of times, some keys, a few coins, a dice, and some postage stamps. Over it were some old sandals made of palm fronds; he must have worn them until he had made his escape. Dawlish closed the locker and went and made coffee and ate some biscuits.

When Harrison and the others came back, he was waiting in front of the big parking lot, in the shade. Harrison's expression gave his report for him.

'Nothing?'

'Not a single diamond stored away,' Harrison said as if disgusted. He was frowning, and his thin features reminded Dawlish vividly of Donovan. 'We found about two hundred in the wreckage, that's all. That was what Parkin and Mason expected to get away with. Still sure we'll find the big supplies?'

'Yes,' Dawlish said.

'Then where?'

'Wade,' Dawlish said, 'Parkin was the leader of this part of the gang. He did a good best to sell us a pup, but he hadn't time. Have you studied a map of this part of the world?'

'So closely I began to go cross-eyed.'

'You can't go north or south—it's impossible. You can go west and eventually you hit the Skeleton Coast, but that's patrolled so tightly by U.D.D. and the individual diamond companies that no one could hope to get away without being spotted. Parkin and Mason planned to get away and to be on the run so that we would be chasing them or on the lookout for them—thinking they had all the diamonds or knew where they were.'

When Dawlish paused, Harrison conceded, 'It sounds reasonable.'

'If they'd got away in that truck, we would have had good reason to believe that they'd taken the loot with them. We now know they only had a tiny proportion of it. We know it isn't here. So where is it?'

Harrison was frowning.

'Are you saying it never was here?'

'I should be surprised if it was.'

'I wish I had your kind of mind,' said Harrison. A few days ago he would have scoffed; now he was obviously half convinced. 'What would be surprising about it? It's a perfect hidey-hole, hundreds of miles from anywhere, derelict, almost forgotten except by the odd prospector looking for gold or some other metal. Name me a better place.'

'It's all right if you know you'll never be found,' Dawlish argued. 'Directly anyone suspects it, it loses its attraction. It's a difficult place to get to but a damned sight more difficult to get away from. A few helicopters searching the area would put paid to any chances of escape.'

'You still make it sound reasonable,' conceded Harrison. 'But I'm not with you.'

'Apart from the wisdom of using this particular spot, would you keep all those diamonds in any one place?'

'Well, well,' Harrison said. 'So they've been selling them or distributing them abroad.'

'They cut all they could here,' Dawlish said. 'Say twenty a day or something over three million pounds' worth a year if the diamonds were worth about five hundred pounds each. I'd say they brought supplies here for cutting, smuggled the cut stones out to their regular distributors, and brought in new uncut stones.'

'A conveyor-belt process,' Harrison said. 'It's logical, but I'm still not sure that's the way it happened. In any case the stones had to be kept somewhere.'

Dawlish said, 'Exactly.'

'Don't be so damned smug! What's up your sleeve?'

'Wade,' Dawlish said gently, 'you're so busy looking at the woods that you can't see the trees right under your nose. We know that Parkin and Mason knew this desert better than anyone else. We know they kept coming into it on their prospecting treks. We know that there are other men in Kangarmie who go out prospecting regularly. We know they talk of Kangarmie as a town of prospective widows.'

Harrison exclaimed, 'Kangarmie!'

'Where else?' asked Dawlish. 'The place Parkin and the other prospectors were always coming back to. Why shouldn't they? It was home. They'd come back for a few days or a few weeks and then go off again taking with them another lot of diamonds for cutting. Who would suspect a fortune hidden in a ghost town like Kangarmie? Out in the desert, yes, but not there.'

'All I need to satisfy myself is to see the diamonds,' Harrison said. 'If you're right, Parkin and Mason led us out here, did the damage to that road, using the bulldozers and the dynamite from here—and then tried to make it look as if all the loot had once been here.'

'That's the way I see it,' Dawlish said. 'There's one thing you don't know, Wade.'

'There's a hell of a lot I ought to have known.'

'Isn't there always, with us all?' asked Dawlish dryly. 'The particular thing you don't know is that the Land-Rover blown up on the desert was accidental. They'd used some old land mines, left here when the area was used for desert-warfare training during the war, for blasting the road so we couldn't get by. They thought we would turn back. When we saw how bad it was, they thought we'd be even more sure we had to look for the diamonds out here. They left a land mine unexploded.'

'Did Parkin tell you this?'

'Near enough,' Dawlish said.

Harrison ran his hand across his sweat-rimmed forehead.

'I said it once before and I'll say it again. When I see the diamonds at Kangarmie, I'll believe everything you say. Right now I only half believe it.'

Dawlish gave a curious kind of laugh, but before he could

speak Della appeared, hurrying, carrying a letter in her hand. Traces of tears showed in her eyes, but at this moment excitement drove everything else away.

'Pat,' she said, glancing at Harrison but taking no notice of him, 'here's a letter you ought to have.' She thrust it towards him. 'Parkin and Mason and some of the other men from Kangarmie used to bring more uncut diamonds here for cutting. Nigel says he keeps trying to find out where they get them from. He isn't sure, but he knows they always brought them after they'd been home, so he thinks they're in Kangarmie.'

After a short pause Harrison exploded.

'Well, I'll be damned!'

Della looked at him in surprise, but she wasn't interested in Harrison, and obviously she had something else on her mind.

'How soon can I get to see Nigel?' she asked.

Harrison answered her.

'You can get to Kimberley in a few hours from now, after the major and I have been dropped at Kangarmie. Eh, Major?'

Dawlish said: 'Yes, of course. Della, I hate to say it, but we'll need to read those letters in case Nigel's said anything which will help us find all the criminals.'

'I see that,' she said simply. 'I'll leave them at my house. Will you stay there while you're in Kangarmie?'

'Yes,' said Dawlish. 'Gladly.'

'Pat,' said Harrison, when they were in the helicopter an hour later, 'you don't seem as confident as you were.'

'I'm confident we'll find the uncut stones in Kangarmie,' Dawlish said. 'But we won't know even then how they're distributed and sold, will we? We'll have finished half the job, that's all.'

CHAPTER XIX

HOARD

Ma Parkin waddled out of the store when she heard the helicopter and watched it as it landed. Everyone who lived in Kangarmie heard the engine and appeared on stoep or at door or window to see whatever there was to see—Ma, whose husband was seldom home, Mrs. Cratton, who waited interminably in her rocking chair for the son who came home from time to time, other women, old and young, whose husbands, sons, and lovers spent so little time at home, so much looking for a fortune which never seemed to get nearer.

Or so everyone said.

Now there was anxiety in every eye as they watched the man-made insect hovering before it began to settle. Soon the sound of the police cars, a new feature of the town, broke the silence created when the helicopter's engine stopped. Dawlish and the American were at the back of the car, and the Buckingham policeman was driving.

Ma Parkin was at the counter of her shop when Dawlish and Harrison entered. Two children who had been at their favourite game of petrol-pump climbing followed Dawlish, who pointed soberly at Ma and put a shilling on the counter.

'Give the children an ice cream, Ma and tell them to come back later.'

The woman's eyes narrowed. She obeyed, watching all the time. The children hurried out; from the door one called: 'Thank you!'

'Dankie!' called the other.

Ma said in a cracked voice: 'It's Jacob. What's happened to my Jacob?'

Dawlish answered, very clearly, very positively, 'It was over very quickly, Mrs. Parkin.'

Her work-reddened hands rose to her big, soft breasts.

'Over,' she whispered. The colour faded from her cheeks as the word came. 'So he isn't coming back.'

Gently Dawlish said, 'I'm afraid not, Ma.'

She looked at him in much the way as Parkin had often looked, as if she were searching for something beyond her range of vision.

'Were you there?'

'I was very near.' When Parkin's wife waited for him, Dawlish went on: 'He wasn't running, Ma. He thought he was going to win.'

'Did he, then? He didn't know he was beaten, did he?'

'No, not for a moment.'

She was smiling, not trying to smile, but actually smiling.

'He never knew when he was beaten, Jacob didn't. He never gave up. Not once in all the time I knew him did he give up. It was quick, you say?'

'Very, very quick. He pressed the self-starter of his car and there was an explosion. He didn't know what was coming. He was on his way back to you.'

For the first time tears shimmered in her eyes. She said nothing but lowered her hands and rested them on the counter.

On either side were stacks of canned foods; behind her were shelves laden with all the goods sold here in Kangarmie.

'Ma,' Dawlish said, 'after he died, we found out what he had been doing.'

She kept silent.

'Where are the other diamonds?' Dawlish asked very gently. 'As soon as we know that we'll be able to stop worrying you.'

She stared at him as if she didn't understand, but she did. She was silent for a long time, then moved towards the flap in the counter and came through. She went to the window and looked out. All there was to see were the two derelict pumps and the one newly painted pump, where two children were sitting as if on a tree.

'Ours are out there,' she said. 'He keeps them in the old Supershell tank under there. Dear Jacob,' she added huskily, 'you thought you were going to win right to the last. Good for you, Jacob.'

'Thank you, Ma,' Dawlish said. 'There's just one other thing I have to know. Where did he get them from? Whom did he send them to?'

She was still smiling, but her lips were puckering.

'I don't know,' she said. 'Jacob always said the less I knew the less I'd say. I could never be trusted to keep a thing to myself, he said. So it's not use asking, Major. It's no use at all. I just know where our diamonds are. I never even asked the others where they kept theirs, but I'll bet there isn't another hiding place as good.'

The diamonds were there, stored in small linen bags tucked away in the big tank beneath the pump which had not been used before. Police, the people of Kangarmie, Dawlish, Harrison, and Van Woelden were there while the pit was opened and the tank emptied.

Then they went to the other houses scattered about the town

which had just received its death blow. They found diamonds, jewels almost beyond price, hidden in every home except the Forrests'. Some were under boards, some in roofs, some buried in the gardens.

All the men were away; only the women watched in fear, and the children in their innocence. The diamonds were loaded into armoured cars to start their journey back to the vaults they came from. When they had started, Dawlish, Harrison, and Van Woelden went to the Forrests' house; before she had gone on to Kimberley, Della had given Dawlish the key.

'Use it as if it were your own,' she said.

It was pleasant, and there was a touch of coolness in the early-evening air.

The first thing Van Woelden had told Dawlish was that the news of Felicity was still good.

'She's actually woken and talked to her nurse,' he said. 'Your man Temple telephoned last night. She doesn't remember anything much, but she wanted to be sure you were all right.'

'Thanks,' Dawlish had said huskily. 'Thanks.'

Now he was thinking how like Felicity Della had seemed in her manner and her wholesomeness.

A boy was in the kitchen, preparing dinner. They were to stay here tonight and leave by helicopter at first light. Dawlish had never known Harrison so quiet. He poured himself a whisky and soda from supplies sent up from the shop, stood broodingly by the window.

'So we've got the loot but not the real men behind it,' he said bleakly. 'What was it you said, Pat? We've done half the job.'

'You will never know a man so pleased as Sir Joel Morpath,' Van Woelden put in. He chuckled into his beard. 'When he learned what had happened the ends of his moustache seemed to curl without being touched!'

'I can imagine,' Harrison said.

'There is a meeting in the United Diamond Distributors board room tomorrow at three o'clock,' Van Woelden went on. 'I promised to send a message tonight if you couldn't get there in time. Is there anything more to do here?'

'Haven't we done plenty here?' asked Harrison. 'Every man in the town's played a part in it. There isn't any town left.'

'It's been living on the diamonds,' Dawlish said. 'It hasn't had a natural life for years. But now it's up to the local police, not to us, thank God!' He stifled a yawn. 'Now all we have to do is find out who had been distributing the cut gems.'

'Which is going to be a big problem for the Conference,' Van Woelden said. 'It was one thing to look for uncut stones. When it is matter of cut and polished diamonds—' He shrugged. 'I think you will find Morpath is satisfied to take the usual chance with that. The losses are not so heavy that they cannot be absorbed.'

Harrison said, 'There's a question I'd like answered.'

'Wouldn't we all?' Dawlish asked almost flippantly.

'Don't tell me you haven't wondered about it too.'

'It depends what it is.'

'Uncut stones were reported from five different places. Remember?'

'London, New York, Sydney, Hong Kong, and Tokyo,' Dawlish responded.

'So it's on your mind too.'

'You mean, why should they begin to sell uncut stones if they're doing very well with the cut diamonds?' Van Woelden pulled at his beard. 'I have wondered, but do we need any reminding of the greed of thieves?'

'Was it greed?' asked Dawlish. 'According to Nigel Forrest's letters'—he pointed to a box in the middle of the table—'he's been cutting and polishing these stones for two years and more.

If he simply said so, I'd question it, but he didn't write those letters to fool anyone. They wouldn't let him post them. He just sat and poured his heart out to Della. So for two years or more they've had a steady market. What was the total, Wade?'

'You guessed a value of three million pounds' worth. You couldn't have been far wrong.' Harrison tossed down the rest of his drink. 'I know, I know. Why start putting uncut stones on the market?'

'For more money,' reasoned the Dutchman. 'They knew the moment Forrest arrived here alive that the end of the road was in sight. They couldn't cut and polish more diamonds. They decided to start selling for what they could get.'

'Most of the uncut stones were still here,' Dawlish objected.

'I don't understand you, Pat,' Van Woelden said. 'The number of stones doesn't affect the principle of selling all they could for what they could get.'

'Certainly it doesn't,' Dawlish admitted. 'But that isn't how they've worked in the past. It's been a deliberate long-term plan.'

'Why are you so stubborn? The game was up after Forrest got back. They tried to kill him and failed, so an entirely different situation faced them.'

'Pat,' said Harrison, 'you mean that they had to run true to form even in an emergency?'

'That's how it seems to me, yes. They might speed things up; they might even change their methods, but the over-all policy would be the same.'

'To fool us,' Harrison put in.

'As over the old mine, yes.'

'There was another way,' Harrison said. 'They fooled U.D.D. in a big way by beating the foolproof security arrangements. Does that fit in with your reasoning?'

'Yes.'

'Then how could they fool us with the uncut diamonds?' demanded Van Woelden almost impatiently. 'Are you two inventing complications, or am I getting to old to comprehend? The affair looks straightforward. We have to find the distributors, but that need not alter the principle that the principals wanted to get in as much cash as they could before they had to close down.'

'I think that's how they hoped we would reason,' Dawlish said.

'How else can we?'

Harrison was pouring himself another whisky.

'They fooled us once by leading us to the old mine so that we would think the big cache had been there but was removed before we arrived. They fooled us by making us think they had a lot of workers at the mine, whereas the men from Kangarmie worked there in stretches—some left the mine just before we arrived but didn't come straight back here. They're still in the desert. The major means that they're probably fooling us again.'

'But the uncut diamonds were put on these markets!'

Harrison sipped.

'Your turn, Pat.'

Dawlish said mildly, 'I keep thinking of Van Diesek.'

'Ah.'

'All the trouble he had in persuading his superiors to let him come to us,' Dawlish said. 'We put it down to a combination of a feeling of self-sufficiency on Pretoria's part and the feeling of isolation South Africa has politically. The ostensible reason was that they were satisfied with their own security measures. How did they really measure up, Wade?'

'Now that Morpath's not here I can tell you. Grade A.'

'Couldn't you fault it?'

'Not seriously. Except that it didn't work. The rules and

regulations really are—heck, maybe I should say they really seem to be foolproof. The mechanism of the vaults is bang up to date. If I were advising a bank on how to put in a security system, I wouldn't advise much different. Yet it's failed over the years.'

'Obviously, because of some flaw you haven't discovered,' said Van Woelden.

'A weak link,' Harrison mused. 'Human, too.'

'That is most likely.'

'Someone stopped Van Diesek from coming to us because the security measures were supposed to be good,' Dawlish said. 'Someone didn't want them checked too closely in case that flaw was found.'

'But Harrison hasn't found it,' argued the Dutchman.

'Perhaps we're on the way,' Dawlish said. 'Who could influence the authorities sufficiently to prevent the police from consulting us? Who could pull political strings or even carry enough weight for his opinions to be considered valid and convincing?'

Van Woelden went very still.

'Now we're getting places,' Harrison said. 'Go on, Pat.'

'Who would want us to *think* that the principals behind the losses were on the run and beginning to sell the stones for what they could get? And who would be sitting pretty whether the stones were found or whether they were still where he or his agents could get at them whenever he wanted them?'

'Here's another poser.' Harrison couldn't interpolate this quickly enough. 'Who could make a foolproof security system fail more effectively than the men who controlled it?' He moved towards Dawlish. 'There's one answer to every question, and you don't need telling what it is.'

'Morpath,' breathed Van Woelden.

'Sir Joel Morpath, no less,' agreed Harrison with a growl in his voice. 'And don't stand there grinning like a cheetah, Major! You've pointed a finger at him. Now tell us how we're going to prove it?'

Dawlish said in his mildest voice, 'I think I might persuade him to make a confession.'

Harrison banged his glass down.

'Now I know you're a phony!'

'Would it be possible to get evidence?' Van Woelden was still shaken, and his cheeks, the only part of his face which showed, were very pale. 'We would have to amass absolutely irrefutable evidence. We would be blocked at every turn— Morpath must be one of the most powerful single individuals in the country. *If* you're right, we would have to move with extreme care, Pat. If we overstepped the mark, if we made charges we could not substantiate, we would be in a very bad position. The Conference is beginning to win the confidence of a great number of police forces, but a major mistake would undo a great deal of that confidence. You don't need telling that.'

'No,' said Dawlish. 'That's why I have to tackle Morpath alone.'

'But you are one of us. You are the presiding chairman. You are the Crime Haters.'

'Wade here doesn't think so,' retorted Dawlish quietly. 'The newspapers didn't think so when we arrived. They put the spotlight on me.'

'I'll say they did,' interpolated Harrison.

'I tell you that if you make a mistake it is a Crime Hater's mistake, not yours alone.'

'You would have been right not very long ago,' Dawlish said. 'But remember the trend of a lot of questions, here and in London? Was this a matter of personal vengeance because of my wife? I said no. That was at least half true. But if I try to break

Morpath down, and if I use measures no policeman should, then my thirst for vengeance will be blamed, not the Crime Haters. I would have to withdraw from the Crime Conference and resign from the Yard, but that wouldn't harm anyone much—except me.'

Harrison was leaning against a table, glass in one hand, broad smile on his face.

'That's the major,' he exclaimed. 'Isn't he right, Van?'

'There's another thing,' Dawlish said. 'I killed Donovan, remember? The man who might have been a vital witness.'

'Don't bring that up now,' Harrison protested.

Van Woelden said slowly, painfully: 'Think you might be right, Pat. I do indeed.' After another pause he added: 'You know the risk you're taking, don't you? If you fail, you may well break your whole career. And I know how much that means to you.'

Dawlish would never know how much his expression was like Jacob Parkin's as he answered: 'If Morpath is the man, we've got to break him. You're quite right when you say it will be almost impossible to prove any case we try to make. If he isn't the man, I'm wrong. I'll back my judgment. What time did you say Morpath is expecting us?'

'Three o'clock,' replied Van Woelden.

'I know it will be more than Wade can bear,' said Dawlish, 'but I think I ought to go to see Morpath an hour ahead of time. Alone.'

CHAPTER XX

ACCUSATION

'Major Dawlish, I cannot tell you how deeply grateful I am,' Sir Joel Morpath came from the other side of his beautifully polished desk. He was smiling; his moustache looked almost as if it had been stuck on; his right hand was outstretched.

Dawlish chose that moment to take out his cigarette case. If Morpath realised that it was a deliberate evasion of a hand-shake, he gave no sign. There was perhaps a slight lessening of his cordiality, but that might have been Dawlish's imagination.

'I confess that I did not expect such remarkable results,' Morpath went on. 'Quite remarkable and outstanding. Do sit down.' The armchairs in front of the desk were capacious and comfortable. 'Mr. Van Woelden told me from the beginning that he had great confidence in you. He also told me that nearly every senior policeman in the Crime Conference has the same confidence. He even went so far as to say that where crime detection is concerned you actually have a sixth sense, a kind of superior sensitivity.'

'A less generous man would say that whenever I had a hunch, I played it as hard as I could.'

'A kind of gambler in detection, eh?'

'Just as you're a gambler in diamonds, perhaps.'

Morpath sat down behind the desk.

'I don't think I've ever been called a gambler before, Major Dawlish. A business man, but—I suppose you mean my activities on the Stock Exchange.'

'No,' said Dawlish, 'I mean your dealings in diamonds.'

He had not smiled since he had come in. He did not smile now. He lit the cigarette and blew smoke out of the corner of his mouth, so that it did not billow between him and Morpath. Morpath's finely drawn face was now almost expressionless. This was obviously the last attitude he had expected, and he was nonplussed.

Then he smiled, as if with sudden understanding.

'Your American friend Harrison must have been getting at you! I do assure you that I have never had any doubt of the rightness of my policy where diamonds are concerned.'

Already he was on the defensive, although he did not really know what the attack was about. He must realise it soon—if he were guilty. If Dawlish was right. The possibility that he had made a dreadful mistake was vivid in Dawlish's mind. It was too early to be sure, too early to guess how this was going.

'I don't believe you believe your policy is right for the diamond industry,' Dawlish said flatly.

Morpath took a long time to respond, probably as long as it took him to fight down a rising anger. He might well be angry even if he were not guilty.

'I must say that I find that remark offensive, Major Dawlish.'

'You were meant to,' Dawlish said.

It was still impossible to be sure, but he thought he saw anxiety in Morpath's eyes. The anger was still there, but it was easy to pretend to be angry. If he was anxious, then he must suspect what Dawlish was getting at. Again he took his time in answering. When he spoke his voice was perfectly composed, his tone frigid.

'Major Dawlish, I must ask you to withdraw that remark or withdraw from this room until you no longer feel such an attitude is justified.'

He had forced the issue, either out of the confidence of innocence or out of a courage forced upon him by guilt. It was a challenge which could not be evaded. Dawlish was still not absolutely sure of the justification for his suspicions, but he had to voice them now. The next few minutes would tell whether he was right or hideously wrong.

He was staking his reputation and his future.

'Sir Joel,' he said carefully, 'a very fine detective with whom you have worked for many years was murdered in cold blood. Three other South African policemen have been killed in the past few days. A young man was forcibly detained for two and a quarter years and made to work like a slave. My wife was nearly killed. A young woman—'

'Major Dawlish, please don't go on. This is in no way relevant to the matter we are discussing.'

'It couldn't be more relevant,' Dawlish contradicted. 'A young woman was driven nearly out of her mind, and a dozen decent families have been broken up. These are simply the effects one can see at first sight. Are you proud of your part in them?'

'My part!' Morpath drew in a deep breath. 'Are you out of your mind?'

Now the alarm flared up in his eyes, broke through his composure, convinced Dawlish for the first time that he was right. Dawlish felt relief pouring into him as he went on:

'That's what I said, your part in these crimes.'

'Major Dawlish, I must ask you to leave at once, or most reluctantly I will have to call members of my staff.'

'I shouldn't,' Dawlish said. 'Or I'll be talking to the newspapers instead of talking to you. There may be a way you can make some kind of amends. if this is handled discreetly.'

'Quite obviously you are suffering under some delusion, which—'

'Let's stop wasting time,' Dawlish interrupted roughly. 'I know you are responsible for the diamond thefts. I know you prevented the police from consulting the Crime Conference for years. I know you employed Donovan and sent him to London to kill Van Diesek. I'm not guessing—I know.'

The colour was receding slowly from Morpath's face. He was clenching and unclenching his hands as they rested on the polished desk. Except for their breathing and the tick-tick-tick of a clock there was utter silence. Dawlish did not interrupt it and did not look away from Morpath. A tiny beading of sweat showed on Morpath's forehead and glistened on his upper lip, above the black moustache.

At last he said, 'You can't know. It isn't true.'

'I also know why you were so anxious to have Van Diesek killed. He had suspected you for a long time because you were the only man who could overcome the foolproof security system. It was impregnable to outsiders. He went through the whole list of people who could break the system from the inside and had to give them all a clean bill—until he came to you. Only you had access to all the combinations and all the passwords everywhere. Only you could pass on information which allowed people like Donovan, Parkin, Mason, and others to get hold of uncut stones. Only you had the world-wide distribution system at your finger tips and knew where to sell at the best prices. Van Diesek reasoned—'

'He guessed wildly and wrongly. As you are doing.' Morpath had control of his anger but not of his fears.

'He worked on finding the proof for years,' Dawlish said. 'He built it up remorselessly, fact by fact. He knew that it was something which the police in this country would find hard if not impossible to act upon, so he came to the Crime Conference. He came to see me.'

'There was nothing at all in Van Diesek's report to indicate any of this,' Morpath declared.

'Not in the report he showed you before he left.'

'Not in the report he gave to you and which you gave to the Crime Conference delegates.' Morpath stood up. 'Dawlish, I can understand the intensity of your feelings and the intensity of your disappointment at not finding the principals of this series of crimes, but you have gone too far. There is not a single charge that can be justified. Any single one would bring ridicule upon you and upon the Crime Conference.' He paused, but Dawlish only looked at him stonily. 'I took the trouble to telephone London this morning and to inquire about your wife. She shows a further marked improvement. Go home to her. You have the glory of finding the fabulous hoard of diamonds, a very great triumph indeed. Don't spoil it. Don't take the risk of fighting me.'

'Morpath,' Dawlish said, 'you are a murderer, a thief, and a liar. You have betrayed the trust of all the mine-owners, all the shareholders, all the workers whose lives you influence. Your fine speech to Harrison was the speech of a hypocrite who has forgotten all the rules of integrity and business morality. Soon I am going out of this room to give a statement to the press and the police. Sealed copies of it are already with my colleagues—there is no way you can stop it. It is a detailed statement based on the report which Van Diesek made to me verbally and which I had taped in my office. He dared not commit it to paper—'

'No newspaper would publish such libel.'

'Those which you can influence might not,' Dawlish said. 'All the others will be glad to.'

He stood up, stared at Morpath unblinkingly, then swung round. There was no sound behind him. He reached the door, not at all sure what would happen next, a long way from sure he had what he needed.

He touched the handle.

'Dawlish,' Morpath said in a choky voice, 'wait a minute.'

Dawlish kept his fingers on the handle.

Morpath came slowly towards him.

'Dawlish, how much will you take for that statement? How much is it worth for you to keep silent?'

Dawlish turned round very softly.

'How much is it worth to you?' he asked.

Morpath was very pale, very still.

'You may name your own price.'

'So I can name my own price,' Dawlish echoed. He felt wildly exhilarated, but nothing of that showed in his eyes. As Morpath did not speak, he went on: 'A million pounds and your signature on a confession to make sure you can never betray me like you've betrayed everyone else.'

'Two millions,' Morpath said quietly, 'and my word that I will never take any steps against you.'

Dawlish opened the door.

Morpath cried: 'Don't go, Dawlish. We must be able to come to terms. I can't sign my life away, and you know it. I'll do anything else you want, but not that.'

Dawlish pushed the door wider open.

Van Woelden, Harrison, and Colonel Voort, the Chief of Police of Pretoria, were outside. On a table near the door was a tape recorder, in the keyhole a microphone which told its own story.

Morpath did not even move as Voort stepped forward.

'As you rightly imagined, gentlemen, Colonel Van Diesek told me of his suspicions,' Voort said. 'I could not be sure whether they were the result of an obsession with his failure. I had to overcome considerable opposition to his visit to London, but the visit could not have been more justified. Now that we have the taped record there will be no insuperable difficulty to obtaining more details and legal proof. I am deeply indebted to you all.'

Della's face was radiant when she came towards Dawlish in the hall of the small hotel in Kimberley where she was staying. She took his hands and said: 'Nigel is much, much better! He looks almost himself again, and he even made a joke this morning.'

'That's wonderful!' Dawlish sensed her elation and shared it. 'Wonderful!'

'Pat,' she went on, 'need I tell him how beastly I was? We've always told each other everything, but need I tell him that?'

'Not a word,' Dawlish answered firmly. 'Absolutely not a word. You've got to go through life sharing that secret with another man. If you even breathe a word to Nigel. I'll never forgive you.'

She stretched up on tiptoe and kissed him.

She had forgotten so much already, forgotten how near she had been to turning to Mason, for instance.

Mason.

After Parkin, Dawlish felt most sorry for him; he must have lived in anguish while Nigel Forrest had been a prisoner. But he had helped to save Forrest; he *had* saved his life once, as he had Della's. But finally he had come down on Parkin's side, on Morpath's. Love for Della and the struggle with his own conscience must have made torment. One moment saying that the desert road had been sabotaged . . . the next smashing the radio.

'Forget him,' Dawlish said to himself.

It wasn't possible to forget Mason, or Parkin, or Ma, or the women and children of Kangarmie, the women knowing that their men could never escape the law.

Dawlish stepped out of the B.O.A.C. jet liner at London Airport, was escorted through customs, and met by Temple who had a big Jaguar with him. Temple drove as if the gears were made of silk. He said very little, except to congratulate Dawlish and to reassure him.

He drove to the big building on the Embankment, where Dawlish had his flat.

'Not here,' Dawlish protested, 'The hospital.'

'Mrs. Dawlish was allowed to come home this morning,' Temple said. 'She'll need time to become her old self again, but she can convalesce at home.'

Dawlish's heart was full to overflowing when he went into the flat. The bedroom door had been repaired, and the hall looked immaculate. The drawing-room door was open. As Dawlish reached it, Felicity was coming across the room towards him, pale of face, but to him as lovely and desirable as she had ever been.

ABOUT THE AUTHOR

John Creasey, born in 1908, was a paramount English crime and science fiction writer who used myriad pseudonyms for more than six hundred novels. He founded the UK Crime Writers' Association in 1953. In 1962, his book *Gideon's Fire* received the Edgar Award for Best Novel from the Mystery Writers of America. Many of the characters featured in Creasey's titles became popular, including George Gideon of Scotland Yard, who was the basis for a subsequent television series and film. Creasey died in Salisbury, UK, in 1973.

THE PATRICK DAWLISH MYSTERIES

FROM OPEN ROAD MEDIA

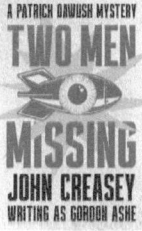  

OPEN ROAD

INTEGRATED MEDIA

Find a full list of our authors and
titles at www.openroadmedia.com

FOLLOW US
@OpenRoadMedia